fiction AND FOLLY

for the festive season

altitude
publishing

fiction AND FOLLY

for the festive season

To Laurell
Merry Christmas!
Love
Linda

fiction by
Linda Kupecek

illustrations by
B. Ian Bazley

PUBLISHED BY ALTITUDE PUBLISHING CANADA LTD.
1500 Railway Avenue, Canmore, Alberta T1W 1P6
www.altitudepublishing.com
1-800-957-6888

First published 2006

Extreme care has been taken to ensure that all information presented in this book is accurate and up to date. Neither the author nor the publisher can be held responsible for any errors.

Publisher	Stephen Hutchings
Associate Publisher	Kara Turner
Editors	Diana Marshall and Lori Burwash
Cover and Layout	Bryan Pezzi

We acknowledge the financial support of the Government of Canada through the Book Publishing Industry Development Program (BPIDP) for our publishing activities.

Altitude GreenTree Program
Altitude Publishing will plant twice as many trees as were used in the manufacturing of this product.

Library and Archives Canada Cataloguing in Publication

Kupecek, Linda
Fiction and folly for the festive season / Linda Kupecek ; Ian Bazley, illustrator.

ISBN 1-55439-237-3

1. Christmas stories, Canadian (English). 2. Christmas--Humor.
I. Bazley, Ian II. Title.

PS8621.U63F54 2006 C813'.6 C2006-904973-4

Printed and bound in Canada by Friesens
2 4 6 8 9 7 5 3 1

Contents

angels in the valley

Just yesterday, the Salvation Army truck arrived to haul away two mattresses, a kitchen table with a wobbly leg, an Oriental rug that had seen better days, and an exercise bike I never got around to using. I suppose I could have put an ad in the *Bargain Finder,* but no matter what, the Salvation Army gets what I have, whether it's a few dented aluminum cooking pots or a whole set of silver-plated flatware.

Sometimes I even buy things at garage sales just to donate them to the Sally Ann. I figure, whatever I can give, the Salvation Army should get. I'm getting on, and the guys who drive the truck always look sort of surprised and pleased to see that I am still around when they lurch into my driveway. I love surprising them every year. Last week, Matt showed me pictures of his new baby, and Eddie invited me to his wedding.

I suppose it all goes back to that Christmas Eve in 1932, when I was 10 years old.

* * *

My Uncle Sandor had recently acquired not only a big, beautiful Ford sedan, which was some feat in the Drumheller Valley during the Depression, but a young wife, just arrived from the Old Country. She had been a governess in Hungary and spoke two languages, German and Hungarian. English might have been handy, but I guess you can't have it all.

Auntie Erzsebet wasn't a pretty woman, but some people would have called her handsome. To me, she always looked as if she was trying hard not to look down on us. Somehow that hurt me more than if she had just hauled back and been nasty and mean.

I guess it was a shock to her to arrive in what was supposed to be the land of milk and honey and discover it was the land of dust and cold and hard times. Uncle's small house was better than most, but it was still a far cry from the chateau in which she had lived in the Old Country.

Everybody was poor, but I always felt as if my family was the poorest. In winter, we put cardboard in our shoes to keep the snow out. In summer, we went barefoot. At Christmas, there was no big tree, no fruitcake, no wrapped presents, no fancy chocolates. We were lucky we had made it through another year.

Of course, it wasn't only us. It was the Depression. All around us, families were living on bread, eggs, porridge, and whatever they grew in their gardens. We lived on a bit of soup and bread. My father always got most of it because he had to work in the mine and bring home the money to feed us. Every night I dreamed of a table covered with roast beef, chicken, and all the cakes and cookies I could eat. When I awakened to the cold bedroom I shared with my four younger sisters, I wondered if I would ever know what it was like to have enough. Enough food, enough clothes, enough anything.

On Christmas Eve 1932, my uncle decided to visit Aunt Teresa and Uncle Paul in Carbon, a coal-mining town on the plateau just out of the valley. He wanted to show off his wife and, for the fun of it, decided to include my mother (his sister), my father, and their five little girls. We were usually stuck in Rosedale, a coal-mining town outside of Drumheller, so when Uncle Sandor asked if we wanted to go to Carbon on Christmas Eve day, of course my father said yes.

Aunt Teresa didn't seem too thrilled when we pulled up in front of their three-room house, their own six kids peeking out the doorway. Now, more than 70 years later, I can understand that she might have appreciated a little notice before receiving four adults and five children. Nobody had a telephone then, so there wasn't any way to confirm a visit, although I suppose my uncle might have found a way if he had thought hard enough.

The first five minutes set the tone of the visit: Aunt Erzsebet carefully wiped off the chair before she sat down; little Andras, the third son of Aunt Teresa, stomped on Zsuzsi's toe (with the usual result of a high-pitched wail from

Zsuzsi); and my father asked Uncle Paul about his job at the mine (from which he had been laid off the day before). Merry Christmas, everybody.

Even though the rest of us quickly ran out of things to do and say, Uncle Sandor stood around talking for the longest time. We were all shifting from foot to foot, wanting to get home, but Uncle wanted to talk, even though it was getting late.

I don't remember much else about the visit except that there were six oranges laid out on the floor by the coal stove. We didn't have anything more exciting in our house, but when we were getting ready to leave, those oranges were looking pretty good to me. If I hadn't been raised a good Catholic girl, with a healthy fear of the priest (and maybe God, too, but the priest was a more immediate threat), I might have wandered a little closer to the nearest of them.

By the time we all piled into the car, it was dark. Uncle and my father were in the front with my sister Ilonka, and the rest of us were layered on top of one another in the back. Auntie Erzsebet looked pretty grim when little Zsuzsi climbed onto her lap, but my mother never complained about the cramped quarters. Mother was pretty stoic. I guess she had to be, with five kids.

It was a bitterly cold night. Dry and black. There was little snow on the ground, and the unpaved roads were hard to tell from the ditch on either side. My uncle must have really wanted to show off, to be willing to drive on such a night. If only it had snowed, the roads would have been light and the air misted with lovely silvery flakes. No such luck. Even the moon and the stars were hidden by clouds.

The drive from Carbon to Drumheller, and then to Rosedale, shouldn't have been so hard. But, just a few kilometres after we left Carbon, the headlights in the Ford dimmed and then went out. My uncle slowed to a stop, embarrassed and annoyed. He fiddled with the controls. He turned off the motor, and started it again. He gently shook the front of the car. Nothing helped. With no lights, the car might go into the ditch. Then we would all be goners. And no priest in sight.

After some discussion, my father and Uncle Sandor agreed on an elaborate signal system, and my father climbed onto the car's hood. Uncle started the car and, driving into the blackness, went right or left depending on my father's arm movements. I'll never forget the sight of my father on the hood, arms swaying this way and that.

None of us said a word. We just watched my father, worried he might fall off the car and get hurt, and watched Uncle, whose hands were clenched tight on the wheel. All of a sudden, my father made an extreme right signal, then a frantic left, but by then, it was too late — the great car lurched off the road into the ditch, gave a little shudder, and lay there at a slight tilt. My father slid off the hood and landed in the ditch beside the car.

Auntie Erzsebet put her head into her hat and started to

cry. The rest of us felt like crying, too, but we held back. She was a newcomer and more easily upset.

I thought my father was dead. Auntie blubbered into her hat. Mother clutched the seat ahead of her and peered over the hood. Finally, Father waved weakly to let us know he was all right. Mother crossed herself in gratitude. The rest of us climbed out into the icy December air. Father and Uncle tried to push the car onto the road, but it was big and the ditch was steep. So we crawled back into the car. No sense in freezing to death on a boulder or two when you could do it in a nice Ford sedan.

Uncle and my father scrambled up to the road, their breath wafting in little icy clouds, waiting for any car they could flag down. The rest of us cowered in the sedan. Auntie kept her hat crushed to her face, and cried and cried. Mother glanced at her — I could tell she was trying to think of something to say that would make her new sister-in-law feel better. None of us had ever seen anybody cry into her hat before. Then Zsuzsi started to bawl, too, and buried her head on Mother's knee.

Down the road, we saw lights. We all peered out of the car, our breath clouding our faces. Uncle and Father waved hopefully. The car lights shone on our faces and kept going.

About half an hour later, another set of lights appeared. Uncle and Father waved their hats. The headlights shone on us for a moment, then picked up speed and left us.

Another three cars passed in the next hour. Maybe they

were afraid to stop, thinking we might be robber barons or something, instead of two men, two frightened women, and five little girls, who were by now crying full throttle. We were making a heck of a lot of noise. Even Auntie Erzsebet, trying to muffle her sobs in her wet hat, wasn't keeping the volume down much.

Maybe the people in the cars were busy. It was Christmas Eve, and they probably had important dinners to attend. While we had no dinner waiting for us. Not that night. Not Christmas Day either. Our biggest treat that evening would be to get out of that ditch.

Two hours passed. Auntie's hat was soaked. Our throats hurt from crying. Mother's face was grim, and she was looking out the window into the dark. I had Zsuzsi on my lap, and my other sisters were leaning on my shoulders. We cried and we cried.

We saw lights in the distance. Uncle and Father stood by the road, ready to try once more. A shiny, black car came toward us, and we knew it was going to be just like the others, flashing on to another important engagement.

But it stopped. And four men in Salvation Army uniforms got out. They looked like angels to me, standing in front of their headlights, the light spraying around them, while they stood, smiling and kind. I had never seen such clean, tidy men in my life.

"Can we help?" asked one, who I guess was the leader.

Uncle and Father explained the situation. Then those

four men, in beautiful, clean uniforms, which most people would not want to get dirty, got behind the car and heaved it onto the road while we watched from the ditch.

Now that things were looking up, Auntie seemed sort of embarrassed by her now-frozen hat. I guess that's why she dropped it as she climbed into the car. Luckily, Ilonka noticed and said loudly, "Auntie, your hat!" Auntie gave her a crooked glare and picked up the hat, but she didn't seem grateful at all. We all squished into the car.

But we still had no headlights.

The men in the uniforms said to my uncle, "Drive ahead of us. We will be right behind you. Our headlights will show you the way."

So our little cavalcade of two cars headed down the road to the Drumheller Valley, the Salvation Army headlights beaming ahead of us. The road into the valley curves and twists, but Uncle kept on the road, his face tense, while we whimpered quietly in the back. Even Auntie was quiet, although I noticed that she was sort of chewing on her hat.

Ten kilometres down into the valley. None of us said a word. We just stared at the road. Yet the lights were always ahead of us.

At the bottom of the hill, Uncle pulled into Mr. Andrews' gas station. Mr. Andrews would know what to do. He could fix anything.

We saw a light go on in the back, so we knew he was coming. Uncle climbed out of the car and waited.

The four men in uniforms pulled up beside us.

As Mr. Andrews came out, Uncle turned to thank the Salvation Army leader. But as he did so, their car suddenly sped away. We all waved goodbye.

"Bless them and that car," said Uncle to Mr. Andrews, nodding after them.

Mr. Andrews looked at him blankly. "What car?"

How could he be so unobservant? Couldn't he see we were waving like crazy at the Salvation Army car that had sped off seconds ago?

But when we looked back, the road was empty. There was no car. Not a trace. Not even the glow of tail-lights.

And that is why I donate everything — from knitting needles to colour television sets — to the Salvation Army.

the bricklayer's party

I've been pals with Connie and Earl since their wild wedding back in 1935, never mind that incident in 1950, when I decked Earl with my trophy for Most Improved Bowler in the hallway of the Silver Pin Bowling Salon. I'm friends with Connie and had no intention of playing Spin the Bowling Pin with Earl in that smelly beer-fumed hallway, knowing that Connie, the gal who'd helped me make 200 pinwheel salmon and egg salad sandwiches for my Dora's wedding, might come walking through that door at the end of the hallway any minute.

But friends get through times like that. Connie and I play bridge with Mary and Yvette every second Tuesday, while Earl goes to the beer parlour with George, Merv, and my Hal.

Their wedding was a real treat. They were arguing at the altar, and the minister finally told them to stuff it or he was going to take a hike and they would still have to foot the bill for the church, the Hammond organist, and the reception. So they got married and I figured they were as happy as any of us.

But it was their annual New Year's Eve party that Connie and Earl were famous for. It was *the* event of Sylvan Lake, Alberta. If you weren't invited, you obviously weren't in the right circles. Lots of folks joined the Silver Pin Bowling Salon hoping to get an invite. Of course, Hal and I went every year. Hal sort of tolerated Earl but he really liked Connie. I couldn't stand Earl but I loved Connie, and I never could forget those 200 (217, to be exact) pinwheel sandwiches that we made together on a sweltering July afternoon, when everybody else I knew was busy washing their hair or watching the signal pattern on the television.

Connie sure knew how to throw a party. She would use a big tin washing tub as a punch bowl, tossing in whatever crossed her path, to make sure people had a good time. I know folks who were in bed for days after those parties because of that punch bowl, but they never regretted a minute of it.

For the choosier drinkers, Connie had a bar with vodka and orange juice, rye and Coke, and gin and tonic. Many was the time when Connie and I would sneak off to the back deck and sit with our gin and tonics and crab about our men or exchange health and beauty tips. Except for New Year's Eve, I didn't drink much. But I knew my Alberta Liquor Control Board brands and I knew my beauty products. Me being a manicurist, sometimes we would get caught up in long chats about nail polish and such. Once I even gave her a manicure in –35 degree Celsius. Connie loved how I did her nails. "Doreen, you're the best," she always said, giving me that little wink that told me she thought I was the cat's meow.

The night of The Party — I think it was about 1955 — things started out grand. Even one of the town bigwigs showed up early in the evening for about five minutes, which raised Earl's stock considerably in the bowling salon. I could tell by the way Merv and George backed off into a corner and looked real unconcerned and disdainful that they were impressed. That's the way with Alberta folk. We don't like to kowtow.

For the first part of the evening, everything seemed to be going great. Mary, George, Al, and Irena showed off some terrific Ukrainian dancing. Maybe George might have been a bit more careful and not clipped Earl's stuffed pheasant with one of his high kicks, but, heck, Earl was in the kitchen arguing with Vladimir about the hockey game, so he was none the wiser. I sort of wish the feathers hadn't landed in my hair. I had paid $5.50 at High Five Beauty Parlour for my 'do, and unfortunately the bits of the bird that Earl had kicked off glued themselves to my hair. Guess it was the hairspray. But what the hey, it was New Year's Eve. I thought I carried it off pretty well, looking as if the feathers were there on purpose.

A couple of hours into the evening, just when Yvette and I were taking bets on who would crash to the floor first, Merv or Vladimir, we heard a huge ruckus in the kitchen.

"You lousy, two-timing, short, # %&* excuse for a husband! Get out of my house!"

Of course, we all knew that was Connie talking. Even if we hadn't recognized her voice, we all knew that Earl had an eye for anything female that walked and talked. (Okay, for Earl, the talking wasn't that important.) And I have it on good authority from a few disappointed ladies in Sylvan Lake that the "short" was accurate.

"*Your* house? Just who built this house?"

Earl had put a lot of blood, sweat, and tears into that house. And I should mention it was a real nice split-level with upstairs, downstairs bath, lemon yellow appliances in the kitchen, and a pink bathroom. Everything the way Connie wanted it. But then, Connie had worked as a town clerk for 10 years to help pay for it, and she had only quit when Earl insisted he wanted a stay-at-home wife to make his life complete.

Connie and Earl had always seemed like a happy couple to the rest of us. But then, we all had our problems, and I guess we just didn't take the time to read the warning signs that peeked up over the years. The little tiffs, the quarrels, the time Connie accidentally ran over Earl's precious motorcycle with the Ford station wagon. How were we supposed to know? I was busy with beauty school, and with my Hal, and then my Dora, and didn't really think much about what was going on with Earl and Connie.

Lately, I'd been wondering why they stayed together —

sometimes you just start thinking about marriages. Like me and Hal. Seems like so long since we really cooked together. You know what I mean. I'm not talking about the kitchen. I guess people sort of settle into a life together, and you find out that work, bills, and that darned driveway that cost a mint and never did sit right get in the way. But Hal and I were still a good match. Not like Connie and Earl.

So why did they stay together? Of course, there were the kids, the sort of excuse that was real handy when you didn't want to hire a lawyer even though the kids kept leaving divorce lawyers' business cards all over the house. The kids were camping out at their pals' homes that night, lucky for them.

Maybe it was that Connie and Earl were used to each other. There is always something sort of comforting knowing that you can figure out what is going to happen day to day.

Maybe it was the house. They had put so much into that house. Everybody knew that if they ever split, there would be a big war over the house. Those appliances and that bathtub, to say nothing of the rec room with the wood panelling and the duck wallpaper. Nobody wanted to be around for the war over the house.

Turns out, we all were.

Even though we were a good six metres away, Yvette and I instinctively ducked when we heard something hit the kitchen wall.

"Get out of my house!" screamed Connie.

"Get out of *my* house!" screamed Earl.

The rest of us looked around, saw there was a lot of liquor left, and decided against leaving, even though, I guess, if we'd been thinking, we would have just skedaddled away and headed to Mario's Pizza House to finish the evening. Naaah. We all hung in there, like people who just had to see the end of the scary movie, even though they knew better.

"This house is half mine!" yelled Connie.

I wondered if I should go into the kitchen and try to smooth things over, but, to tell you the truth, I was scared.

Then we heard a frightening growl from Earl that put some starch in my backbone. Connie was my friend, and I shouldn't be in the living room, standing around like a dodo, while my friend was fighting for her house.

So I slammed down my drink and stomped to the kitchen door. I could tell from the intake of breath all around the living room that everybody thought I was a standup gal for doing it — or maybe they were just afraid I might collar one of them to come with me.

I swallowed hard and pushed myself through the door, painted yellow to match the appliances.

I was alone in the kitchen with Connie and Earl.

They were staring at each other, breathing hard. There was a ham, which must have cost at least six dollars at the grocery store, lying on the floor next to Earl. Wow. For Connie to throw a ham, she must have been real steamed. The ham, on the other hand, was real cold and wonked out of shape.

I made a note to myself to stop Mary from trying to serve it when Connie wasn't looking.

Earl was a barrel-shaped guy with muscles, a face like a radish, a head that was trying real hard to hold on to his last 55 hairs, and a teeny moustache that never went away and never really said it was there. He had a nice rose tattoo on his right shoulder, which always turned a brighter blue when he was drunk. I bet it was as bright as a Christmas tree light tonight.

Connie, on the other hand, was what we all called a "real woman." She was stacked and, even in middle age, had all the right curves and a beehive that meant business. She wore eyeliner with an attitude and was the sort of gal who would elbow aside a creep in a supermarket to keep a kid from getting bashed, and who was even better at rummage sales.

"I own half!" hissed Connie.

"So do I!" hissed Earl.

"Fine," said Connie. "Take your half. Ha. Ha."

Earl stared at her for a long minute. Then he said, very slowly, "Fine. I will."

He turned and walked out the door.

Connie and I stared at each other.

"You okay?" I asked. (I felt like smacking myself on the forehead. Dumb question, Doreen.)

There was a long pause.

"Sure," she said.

Meanwhile, I was listening to Earl's footsteps. I was

praying that I would hear him thumping up the stairs to their bedroom, where he would pass out, and then they would wake up in the morning and pretend nothing had happened. Then we could all pretend nothing had happened and come back next year for the next New Year's bash.

Darn, I heard Earl's heavy footsteps head to the front door. I heard Yvette say half-heartedly, "Earl, how are you feeling?" But of course he ignored her. I heard Merv say, "Earl, buddy, how about we go for a drive?" I heard the door slam, I assume, in Merv's face.

I concentrated on Connie. I expected her to be distraught. I sure would be if I'd just had a blowout like that with my husband. But then, Hal and I never fought. He was too quiet and sweet. If we ever had words, I had to do all the fighting for both of us, and that was no fun. But I didn't know anything about Connie and Earl's private moments, and I just couldn't place a bet on whether this was a minor league tiff or Big-Time Divorce.

Connie was a beautiful woman, even if she was showing the few extra pounds of middle age. Her black bouffant still rode high on her head. And maybe she had a few little vertical lines between her eyebrows and her cuticles were a bit drier than they used to be, but who would notice after a look at her gorgeous skin and dark eyes? I always liked to do her nails a bright fuchsia pink. Tonight they matched her fuchsia pink hostess dress perfectly. I spent nearly an hour on those nails and, I have to say, they were the best of my holiday season.

I was glad it was for Connie, who deserved bright pink nails and everything else that is good and wonderful.

I loved Connie, but I didn't know how to talk to her just then. What do you say? "Oh, Connie, he's such a loser?" But then, Earl wasn't really a loser. He was just a guy. Like so many other guys. Mad and frustrated and afraid. Mostly afraid of losing Connie. Because she was so great, and he was just, well, not so great. But Connie loved him.

I sat awkwardly with Connie. She was my friend, and I would never forget the 217 pinwheel sandwiches, but it was still hard to find the words to say what I wanted to say. I wanted to say that I loved her, that I would love her whether or not she stayed with Earl, and that I wouldn't judge her for either of those decisions. But it was real hard to get those words out of my Sylvan Lake mouth. Plus, you never know when those words will turn into a giant foot in your mouth.

Connie sat at the kitchen table, a nice yellow Arborite that matched the appliances perfectly. She was staring out the window, not really noticing anything. She didn't look very sad.

Just as I was about to rummage around in my mind and find something reassuring to say, something along the lines of "I love you, he is an idiot, you should go to Vancouver and find a sexy sailor and live with him, he would love your bouffant, and by the way, I'll give you a free manicure next week," or else maybe "What do you think of the feathers in my hair?" ... there was a *thunk* at the front door.

Connie and I jumped. She knocked over a bowl of pretzels, and I stuffed two of them into my mouth right away to hide my nervousness. Then there was some clattering and thumping in the front hallway. I heard Merv say, "Hey, Earl, what are you doing?"

Then I heard Earl say something obscene, which I won't repeat here.

I heard George say, "Hey, Earl, that's not necessary."

And I heard another obscene sentence from Earl.

I looked at Connie — she was ready for battle. Putting her manicured hands on the kitchen table, she pushed herself up. I followed her into the living room.

Earl was in the foyer. There was a dusting of snowflakes on his head, and he was surrounded by bricks. Hundreds of bricks. He had his mortar and mortarboard and looked like a comic book hero ready for battle. There was dust rising around him like in one of those epic movies. It took me a moment to realize those bricks were just darned dusty and that Earl hadn't turned into some sort of gladiator. Nope, poor Earl just looked middle-aged and sort of desperate, dust rising around him and he had a glazed but real determined look in his eyes.

The other guests stood around, trying to look like innocent bystanders.

"Earl," I said, "what are you doing?"

"What do you think I'm doing?" he shot back. "We're dividing the house. So I'm dividing the house, Featherhead." I thought this comment was completely unnecessary.

And then he set into his work. He was a bricklayer. I guess I didn't mention that. And he started to lay a brick wall through the house. He began at the front door, laying bricks, slathering on mortar, working as if there was a pack of Dobermans coming after him.

Connie stood for a long moment, looking at him. I couldn't tell from her face what she was thinking. Me, I would have been screaming, "Are you crazy?" But Connie just stared at him with a strange look on her face, and then she turned and went back into the kitchen. I followed, to make sure she was okay.

She was still quiet, and she still had that funny look on her face. She leaned back in a kitchen chair, lit a cigarette, and blew smoke at the ceiling. I couldn't help it — I looked up to see if there was anything interesting up there, from the way she was staring, but all I saw was her smoke.

I leaned through the kitchen door and peeked into the living room. Earl was dividing the house, all right. But the way he was doing it, after a few beers and all, he was getting the living room, the porch, and the foyer. According to his brick wall, Connie would get the kitchen, bathroom, bedroom, and even the stairs to the basement rec room. In other words, Connie wasn't doing too bad. If he kept going, Earl would have to negotiate with her for the use of the facilities.

Brick by brick, he was building the wall, sort of like Poe's "The Cask of Amontillado," which I had read in high school and always found sort of creepy. I peeked out the kitchen door and saw that Vladimir, Mary, Hal, and the rest of them were just staring at him, drinks in hand, trying hard not to look too concerned. Nobody in their right mind would do that to a split-level, not with property prices the way they were.

I leaned back into the kitchen. Connie lit another cigarette and fumbled around for her gin and tonic. As usual, I found myself trying to make conversation in manicure language.

"Next time, how about a nice carmine? Something different? Or maybe a really pale frost?"

Silence. She took a long drag on her cigarette then watched the smoke rise about her head, above the jellied salads she hadn't put out, the smoked meats, the cabbage rolls that were slated to go into the oven, and the platters of cakes and cookies she always served at midnight. New Year's Eve. Beginning of the next year.

I peeked out the yellow swinging door again and saw that Earl had made it to the aquarium — the wall was knee high. He was about three metres from the kitchen. He still had a way to go, but it was looking pretty frightening. He was working fast and breathing hard. I was impressed.

Behind him, like characters out of a Disney cartoon, Merv and George were fidgetting and sending signals in some sort of drunken sign language. Even I could figure out that they were saying something along the lines of "Knock him out and I'll knock down the wall," or maybe "Meet you in Red Deer at Al's Pizza."

Behind Merv and George were the rest of the guests. I guess they just couldn't believe what they were seeing, because none of them were moving or even blinking, not even my Hal, who always moved slowly anyway. They could have been a bunch of lawn ornaments you buy at Woolco. Jeez Louise, were they frightened? It wasn't as if Earl was invincible. He was just a drunken, desperate guy, but, after all, he was the guy who loved Connie.

Wasn't anybody going to do anything? Was I the one who would have to have a showdown with Earl and maybe get decked for my trouble and then I would have a black eye and nobody wants to go to a manicurist with a black eye and then I would lose business and would have to move out to live with my brother on the chicken farm because Hal would divorce me if he thought I was getting into fights at parties, even though Hal was there and should know I was an innocent bystander ...?

Anyway, while all this was going through my head, something amazing happened. Hal, my Hal, the one who tells me never to get involved, brushed past Merv and George and walked right up to Earl. My Hal is a big guy, but because he's so quiet, you never feel afraid of him or anything. He's a pussycat, which is why I nearly fell over when I saw him looking Earl right in the eye.

Hal said, "Hey, Earl, did you see that moon tonight?"

Earl looked at Hal as if he were making a pass at him.

"And the Ryerson girls love to walk in the full moon in

their nakeds. Even in winter. I never seen anything like it." The Ryerson sisters were renowned in the town for their gorgeous shape, but I had never heard *this* about them.

Earl slowly put down his mortarboard and followed Hal to the door like a beagle on the trail. Hal held the door open for him and made some sort of weird movement behind his back with his hand. If he had made it to me at a really boring party, it would have meant "Let's get out of here." But he made it in the general direction of George, Merv, and Vladimir, and as soon as the door closed behind Earl and Hal, there was an explosion of activity.

George ran into the kitchen and grabbed a black plastic garbage bag, right in front of Connie, who just took another slug of her drink and another inhale. He ran back just as Merv pulled off three bricks and threw them into the bag. They started getting a good rhythm going. Merv grabbed three bricks, threw them into the bag, George shook the bag a bit to settle it, then moved into the next position. Of course, after about one minute, they realized the bag was going to break in thirty seconds, so George ran back into the kitchen and grabbed the box from the liquor store, which worked better.

By this time, the rest of the guests had got into the mood and, realizing that one piddly little box wasn't going to work for all those bricks, had formed a sort of brick brigade. Merv would brace his foot against the wall, grab a brick, and pull it off, hand it to the person beside him, who would pass it to the next and the next, through the lineup to the back door, and

Yvette — who had what I finally figured out are what magazines now call "anger management issues"— would heave it into the backyard on top of the strawberry patch. ("Most fun I've had in years," she told me later.)

The blast of cold air from the open door perked us up and kept us going. A fit of giggling took over every now and again. This was supposed to be a serious rescue operation of a nice split-level house, but instead, everybody in the brigade line alternated between hellbent-for-leather brick passing and hysterical giggling. They pretty well had to work around Connie, who was still sitting and smoking. Her glass was empty, but we were all too busy for refills.

Yvette turned out to be the star of the evening, with the supreme style with which she, as the last link in the chain, heaved the bricks into a pile in the garden. I admired Yvette that night. I felt she had made a breakthrough and would never wear beige nail polish again.

Meanwhile, my Hal (my Hal, I say in amazement) was out front with Earl. I never dreamed my Hal, who had never said boo to the cat, would take Earl outside and try to talk sense to him. My Hal is a firefighter but he doesn't have a single tattoo and he never talks dirty like Earl.

By the time the last brick was in the strawberry patch and everybody, exhausted but still in the game, got to cleaning up, the house was looking not too bad. Merv and Yvette were sweeping up, while Mary and I were passing around whatever food had survived the evening. (The cabbage rolls had made their way into the oven, thanks to Yvette.) We just grabbed plates and ate, standing around Connie in the kitchen. There's nothing like an evening of shocks and hauling bricks to work up an appetite.

We were pretty pleased with ourselves. We had done a darned good job of stepping up to the plate and saving a nice split-level house from really being split. But would Connie and Earl split? What was going to happen with their marriage?

It must have been close to midnight, but by this time, nobody cared. Soon we would all have to kiss people we didn't want to kiss just for the sake of tradition. I started to roll my eyes at Hal (as in "Let's blow this pop stand. I've done my duty. The last lifeboat is leaving!"). Hal knew I hated kissing these big-bellied guys and, just once, I would have liked him to take my side, so I wouldn't have to do the knee-in-the-you-know-where routine.

But Hal wasn't around. He was still outside with Earl. *Still outside with Earl.* My heart started to pound. I realized that if Earl had done anything to Hal, even touched a teeny nose hair of my Hal, I would kill Earl. I would pound him with a meat tenderizer mallet and threaten to grill him over a barbecue. I would paint him with violet cologne and tie him up and put him out for the killer mosquitoes to bite. I would stomp on him with my black patent spike heels until he begged for mercy.

Just as I was about to charge out the kitchen door, it

opened. Hal shoved Earl into the room. Their cheeks were red with cold, and Hal had a bit of an icicle hanging from his right ear. Earl sort of staggered, then fell into Connie's lap. Luckily, Connie, being a bigger woman, could take this shock. Earl had a real shiner, almost as good as the one Merv got when he took on the trucker at the Five Mile Café.

"I'm sorry, Connie," said Earl. And knock me over with a feather duster, but Earl was crying. Earl, the tattooed blowhard of all time, was crying. He put his head on Connie's shoulder, and his tears made little blotchy stains on her fuchsia bosom.

I thought Connie would shove him away, but she put her arms around him and said, "I know, honey."

The clock chimed midnight.

The guests started to fade away after that. A few of us hung around to check the stove, the lights, and say our goodbyes. Connie and Earl were all wrapped up in each other and didn't give a hoot.

Merv thumped Hal on the shoulder and said, "Happy New Year. Good job." George shook his hand. Yvette kissed him (and maybe for a few more seconds than I would have liked). And so on.

Everybody seemed to think Hal had done something special. Well, I knew that. My Hal *is* something special. Always has been. I looked at my Hal and saw the guy I'd dated in high school, the guy who always kissed me sweetly on the shoulder when I was blue, and I loved him all over again. I looked at Connie and Earl and got sort of teary-eyed over the way Earl was looking at Connie. And the way she was looking back at him, with her dark eyes sort of misty.

Merv stopped at the door and called out to Connie and Earl (who were deep into what they were doing and didn't care), "Happy New Year!"

Yvette kissed Connie's bouffant. "Happy New Year."

Vladimir grabbed me to plant his usual sloppy kiss on my lips, but my Hal pushed him away with a grin. "Not this year, Vlad." And Vladimir faded away, too. Beat me with a powder puff, it happened.

Yup. And then my Hal leaned down and gave me a kiss that sent a little tremble all the way to my toes. Sort of in a daze, I turned to say goodbye to Connie. But she and Earl were … oh well, you know … Hal and I waited for them to come up for air, and when they did, we said, "Happy New Year."

They smiled back. "Happy New Year. See you next year." And then they got back to what they were doing.

And Hal and I slipped away, into the new year.

Santa's Working Drawings
(A.K.A. "How to Christmas")

There are strange things done 'neath the Arctic sun
By the elves who toil on toys;
Making things with wings and dolls of string
For goodly girls and boys.
But the Arctic gales hid some secret tales
Of espionage, deceit;
When Scrooge the elf took from the shelf
The drawings you now meet.
(WITH APOLOGIES TO ROBERT SERVICE)

The world's most audacious case of industrial espionage occurred in 1844 when a disgruntled elf by the name of E. (Elf #49) Scrooge stole the very plans that Santa used annually to make Christmas. A "How To Christmas" guide for the Arctic handyman, these plans were hidden for decades within the walls of an abandoned igloo at the corner of Portage and Main.

The drawings came to light when global warming drove Winnipeg's temperature to a soaring, searing 1°C.

* * *

Originally, Santa carved his plans on blocks of super-cold ice, but in 1379, when one of the apprentice elves accidentally left the lights on in the storage vault overnight (October 21 – April 21), tragedy struck. (Santa had discovered electricity after the New Year's Eve party in 1353 when he thought it would be "neat-o" to fly a kite in the aurora borealis. Hence, the curly beard ...) This accident, considered the catalyst of global warming, had dire consequences, foremost of which was the extinction of the unicorn, when the unicorn drawing melted clean away. Contrary to popular belief, the loss had nothing to do with Noah.

To prevent further tragic extinctions, Santa tasked a San Franciscan monk, Brother Philonius Photus Copius, to painstakingly transfer the remaining ice carvings to parchment, ensuring that nothing else would be lost to melting or mistakenly used to chill a kegger.

* * *

E. Scrooge, the hapless villain, was not a very good elf. As a result, he was always being assigned to K.P. duty (which in the Olde Norse tongue of the elfin means "Kleanderdeeren

Poopitmessen"). Having had his fill of deer spill and feeling particularly upset with Donner, who after becoming too tipsy, in celebration of a successful run in 1843, did a "poo-boo" (which refers to a particularly odious offering, bordering on offensive), E. Scrooge decided to put an end to his problems by putting an end to Christmas. The vengeful elf stole Santa's working drawings and hid them in the most remote location known to man — Winnipeg — believing that without drawings there could be no more Christmases, no more merriment, and hence no more K.P. duty. This well-documented historic event is chronicled in the Dr. Goose tale, "How the Grouch Stole Christmas."

Fortunately by 1579, Santa had already converted all of the drawings to digital format, storing them on his Orange computer. The computer, based on the abacus, was Santa's primary binary information storage system, wherein data was posted on long rods in the form of "orange" and "no orange." While this system worked well at the North Pole, his laptop got mouldy whenever he travelled to tropical lands.

Once discovered, the original drawings changed hands between unscrupulous paper recyclers and incredulous art historians until they finally surfaced in Calgary, where they were authenticated and subsequently purchased by the local CHUMPS (Calgary History of the Unusual and Museum of Phenomena and Science). In turn, they were eventually made available to this publisher for dissemination to the world's Do-It-Yourselfers for their enlightenment and use.

We trust that you will find these works of use in crafting your own Christmas. It should be noted, however, that Santa has patents pending on the "Christmas Moose," "Super-Duper Christmas Tree Wrap," and "Procrastinators' Xmas Eve D.I.Y. Lifesaver," and has advised us that he intends to defend any infringements vigorously. Otherwise, we wish you a merry Christmas!

FOR SANTA
B. I. BAZLEY,
TUKTOYAKTUK,
2006

PROCRASTINATORS' XMAS EVE

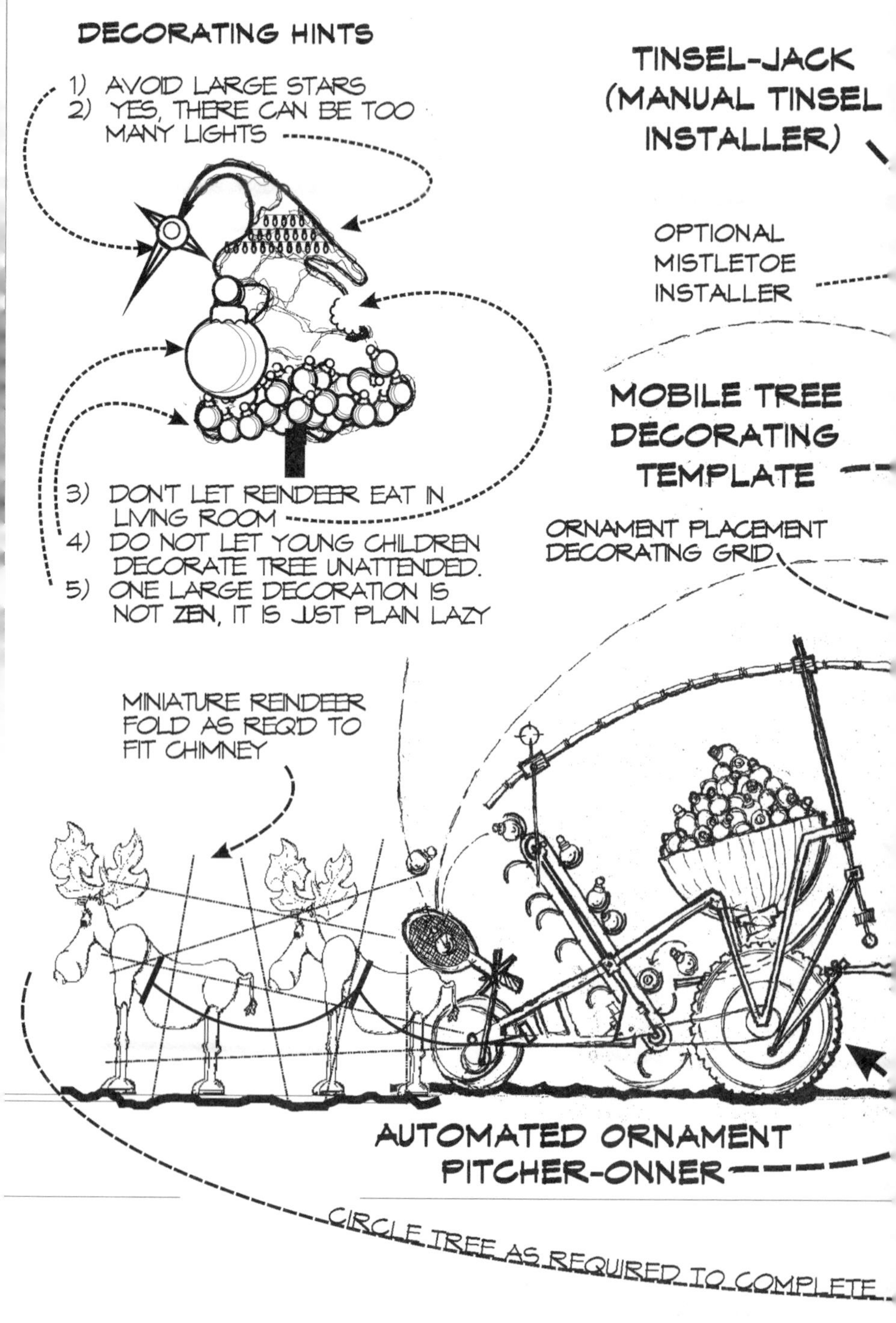

D.I.Y. LIFESAVER

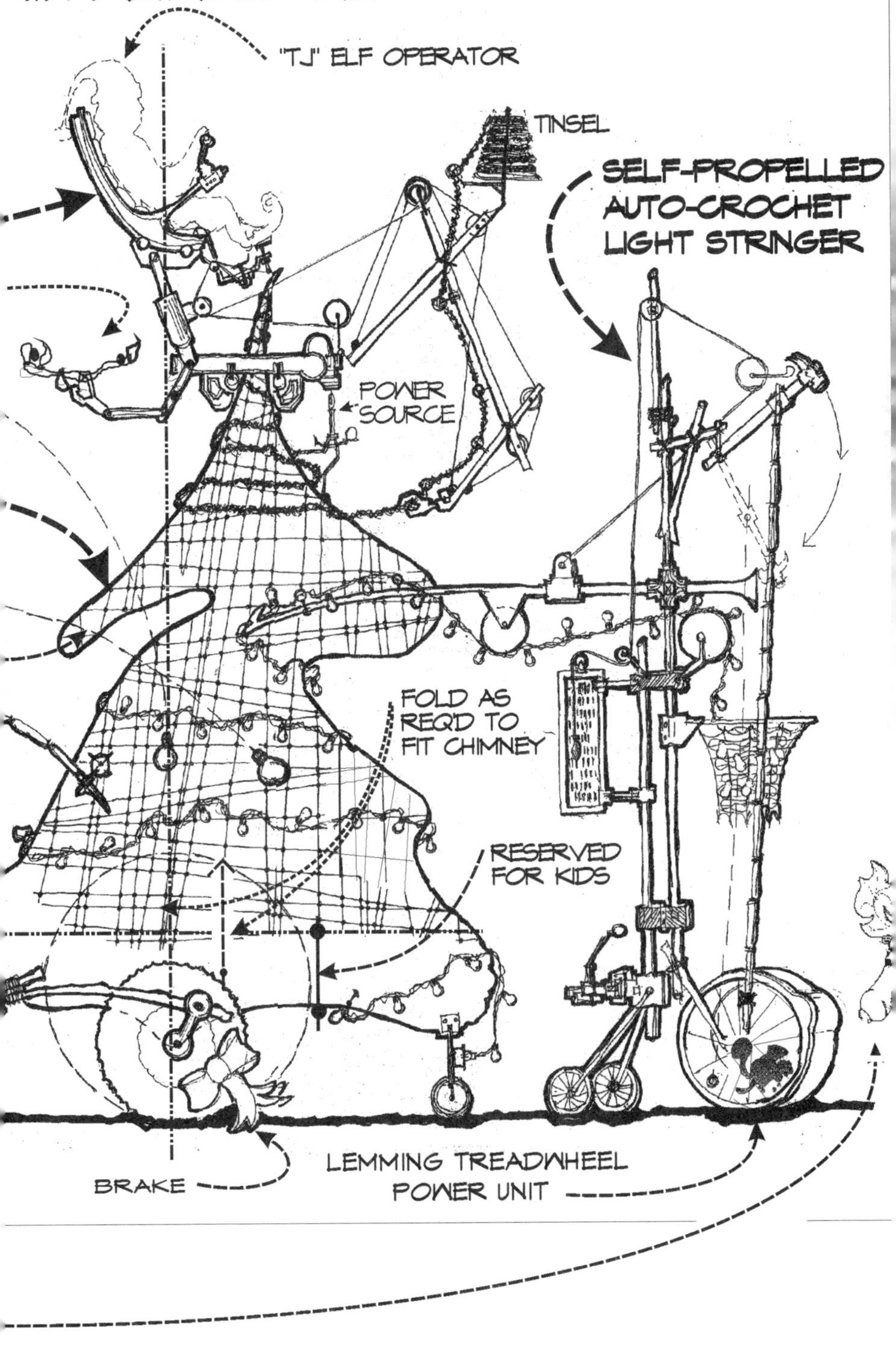

D.I.Y. TREE -IN-A- BOX

PREMIUM UNITS:

* SPRUCE UP FIR PUBLIC DISPLAY
* CEDAR BACK FOR FIRTHER INSTRUCTIONS
* REUSED ANNUALLY BY POPLAR DEMAND
* WE ALL PINE FOR GOOD JOKES

1 ENLARGE TEMPLATE 43,278%

2 USE 43 gal CONTACT CEMENT & GLUE TO

3 3 SHEETS OF G1S PLY 29" x 17'-6" x 3/4"

4 CUT OUT

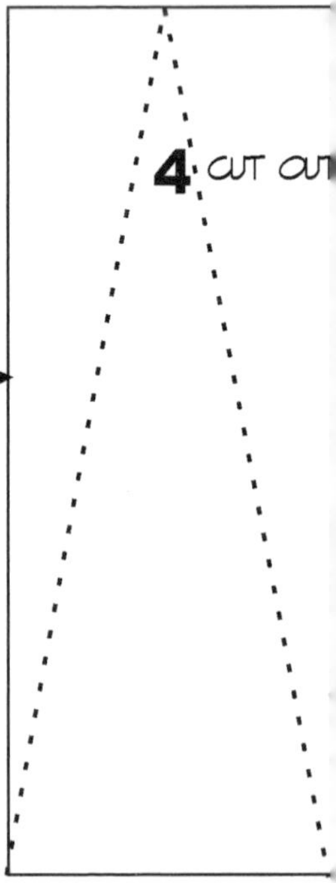

THIS POINT TO TOP

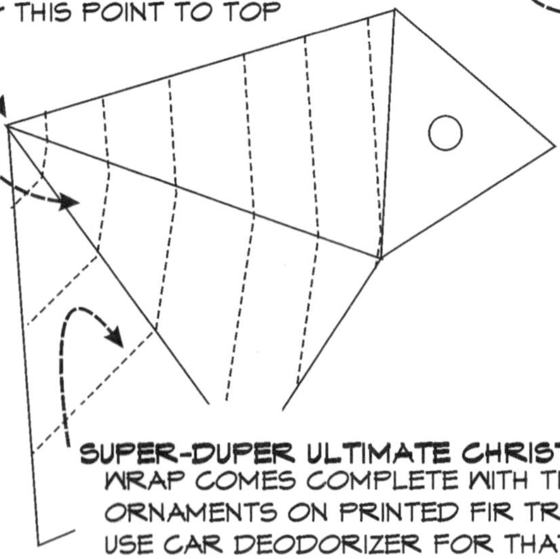

SUPER-DUPER ULTIMATE CHRISTMAS TREE WRAP

WRAP COMES COMPLETE WITH TINSEL, LIGHTS, AND ORNAMENTS ON PRINTED FIR TREE BACKGROUND. USE CAR DEODORIZER FOR THAT "FRESH PINEY" SMELL. ICICLE STYLE WRAP MUST BE KEPT IN FRIDGE.

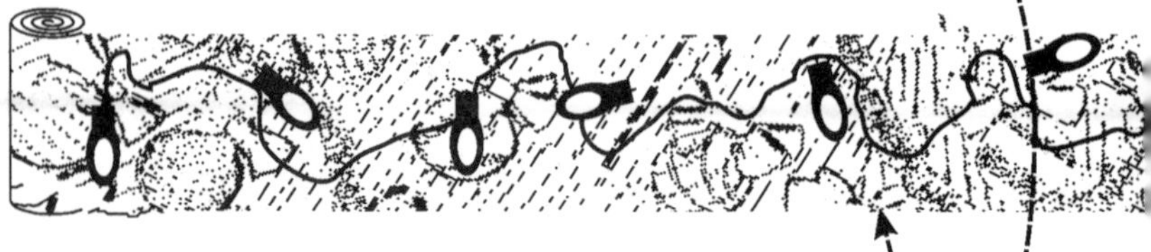

PUT TOGETHER

STAND IN LIVING ROOM

REPAIR CEILING AS REQ'D

WRAP IN SUPER-DUPER CHRISTMAS TREE WRAP

ICICLES SHALL BE: 12" x ½" dia @ 14" c/c VERT. & 2" c/c HORZ. AND COMPOSED OF H²Ho!Ho!Ho!

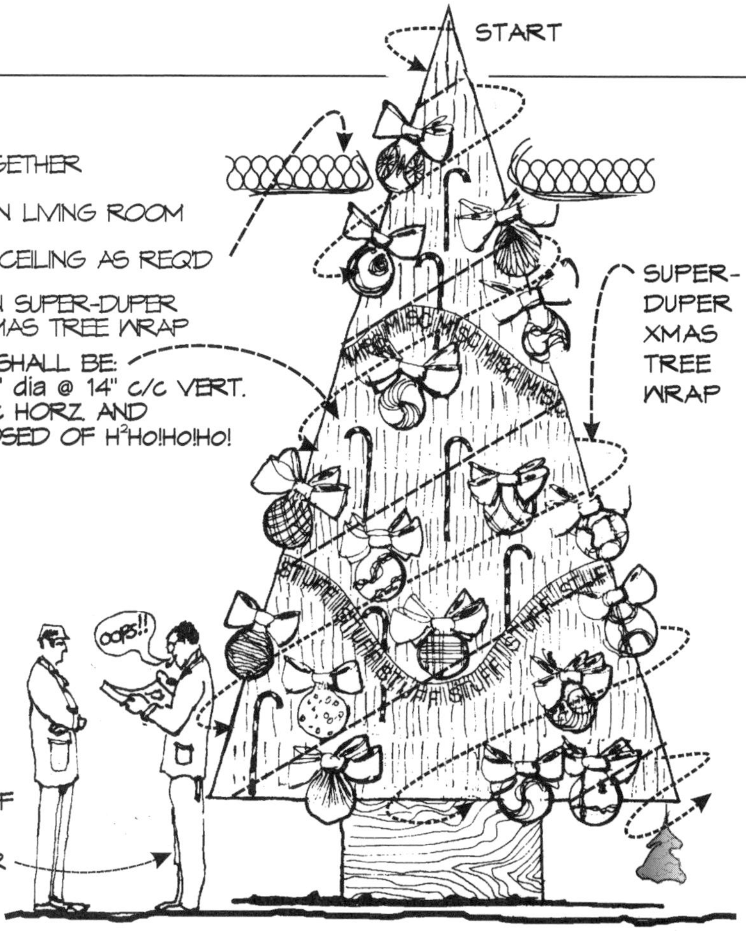

NOTE: Contractor shall enlarge room as required to suit tree, free of charge. Designer is not responsible for anything.

0 DISCARD BOX

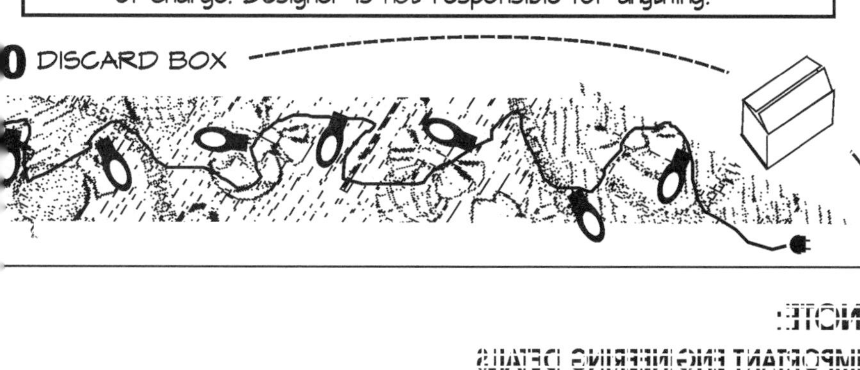

NOTE:
IMPORTANT ENGINEERING DETAILS
ON REVERSE MUST BE FOLLOWED

EDITOR'S SAFETY NOTE: REMOVE LIGHTNING ROD BEFORE LEAPING INTO THE CHIMNEY

FIRE ASSURANCE: You have our assurance that if you set a match to this book it will catch fire.

SANTA'S SUMMER MOBILE MANS

DESIGN BY F. L. WRONG @ the Bahumbug School of Design

NTRACTOR TO USE THOSE COMPONENTS SUCH AS ARE APPLICABLE.

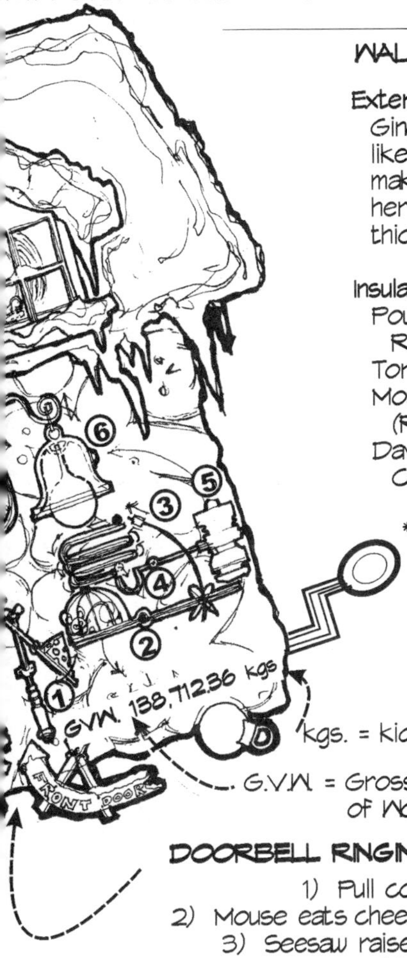

WALL CONSTRUCTION

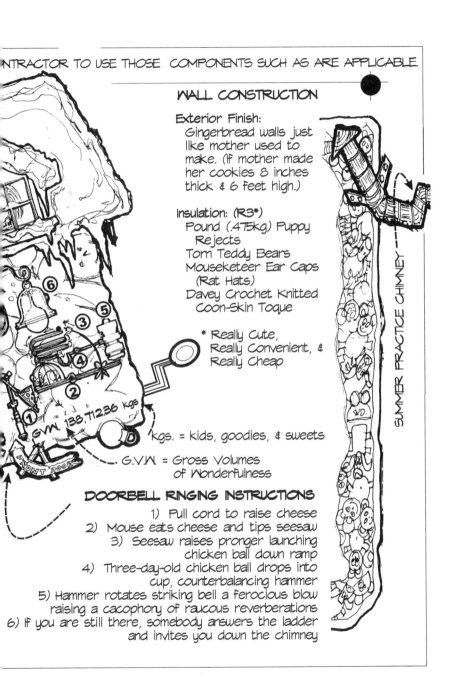

Exterior Finish:
Gingerbread walls just like mother used to make. (If mother made her cookies 8 inches thick & 6 feet high.)

Insulation: (R3*)
- Pound (.475kg) Puppy Rejects
- Torn Teddy Bears
- Mouseketeer Ear Caps (Rat Hats)
- Davey Crochet Knitted Coon-Skin Toque

* Really Cute, Really Convenient, & Really Cheap

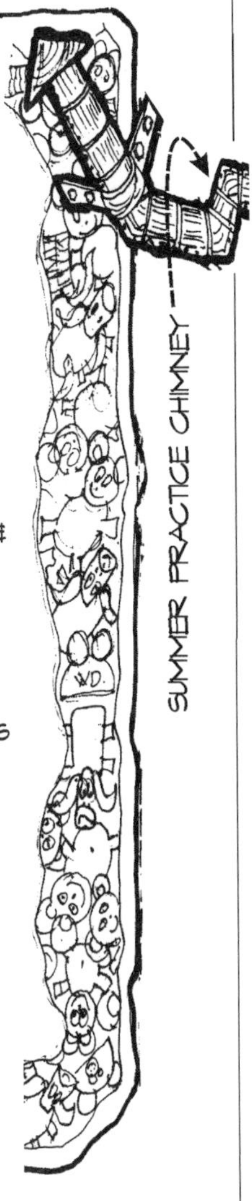

kgs. = kids, goodies, & sweets

G.V.W = Gross Volumes of Wonderfulness

DOORBELL RINGING INSTRUCTIONS

1) Pull cord to raise cheese
2) Mouse eats cheese and tips seesaw
3) Seesaw raises pronger launching chicken ball down ramp
4) Three-day-old chicken ball drops into cup, counterbalancing hammer
5) Hammer rotates striking bell a ferocious blow raising a cacophony of raucous reverberations
6) If you are still there, somebody answers the ladder and invites you down the chimney

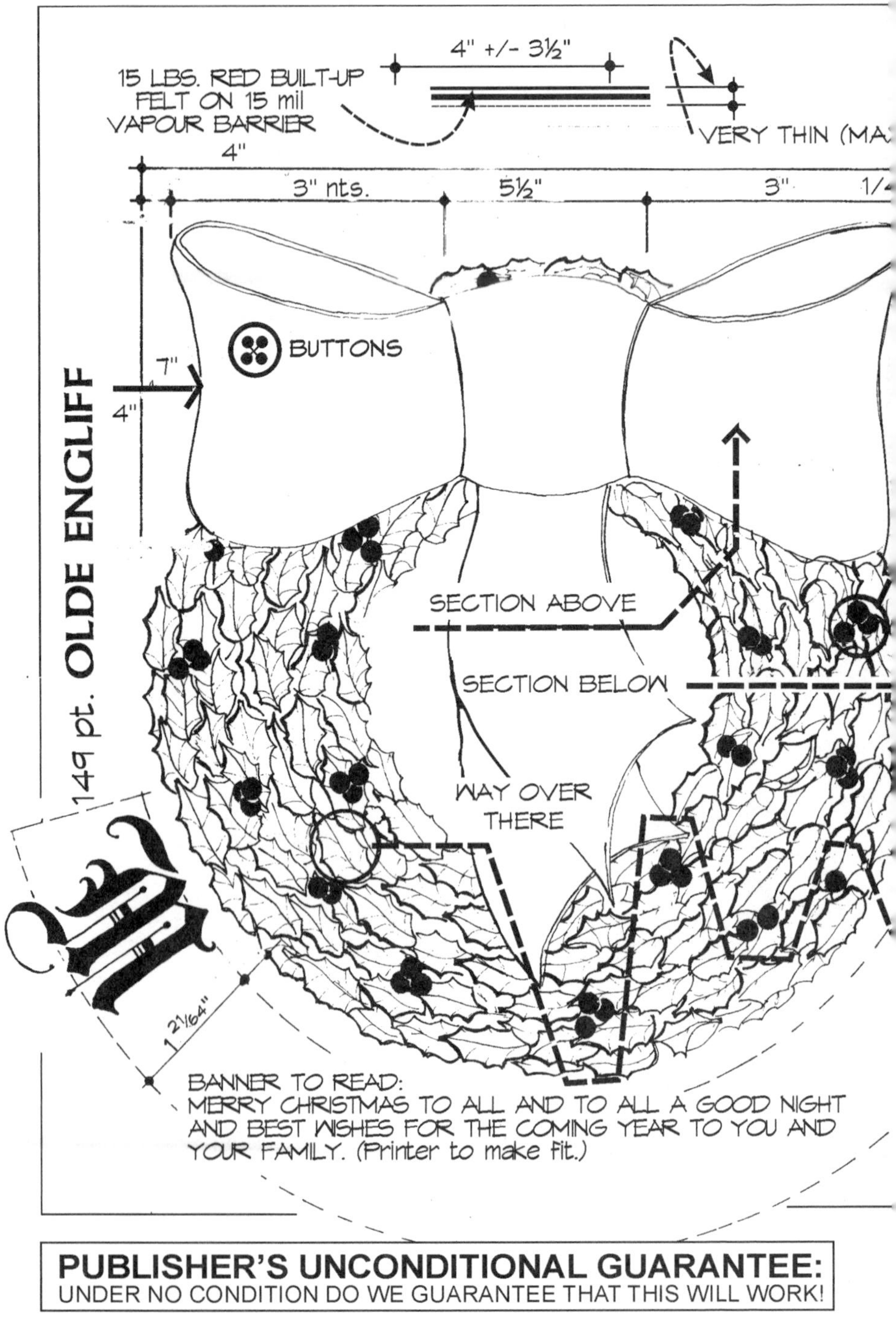

PUBLISHER'S UNCONDITIONAL GUARANTEE:
UNDER NO CONDITION DO WE GUARANTEE THAT THIS WILL WORK!

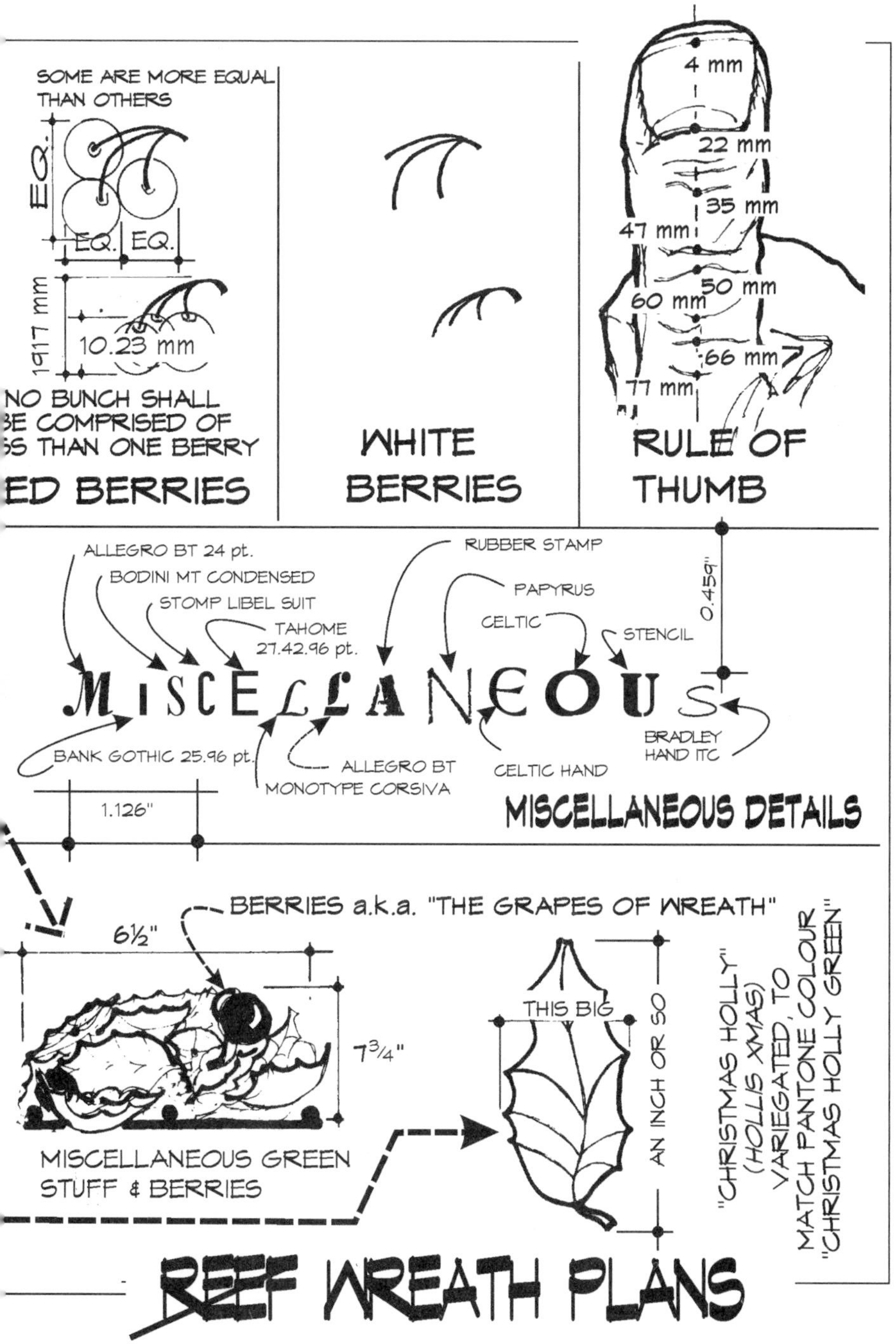
SOME ARE MORE EQUAL THAN OTHERS
EQ.
EQ. EQ.
1917 mm
10.23 mm
NO BUNCH SHALL BE COMPRISED OF LESS THAN ONE BERRY
ED BERRIES
WHITE BERRIES
4 mm
22 mm
35 mm
47 mm
50 mm
60 mm
66 mm
77 mm
RULE OF THUMB
ALLEGRO BT 24 pt.
BODINI MT CONDENSED
STOMP LIBEL SUIT
TAHOME 27.42.96 pt.
RUBBER STAMP
PAPYRUS
CELTIC
STENCIL
0.459"
MISCELLANEOUS
BANK GOTHIC 25.96 pt.
MONOTYPE CORSIVA
ALLEGRO BT
CELTIC HAND
BRADLEY HAND ITC
1.126"
MISCELLANEOUS DETAILS
BERRIES a.k.a. "THE GRAPES OF WREATH"
6½"
7¾"
MISCELLANEOUS GREEN STUFF & BERRIES
THIS BIG
AN INCH OR SO
"CHRISTMAS HOLLY" (HOLLIS XMAS) VARIEGATED, TO MATCH PANTONE COLOUR "CHRISTMAS HOLLY GREEN"
REEF WREATH PLANS

ARCHETYPICAL ELF #1 OF 1

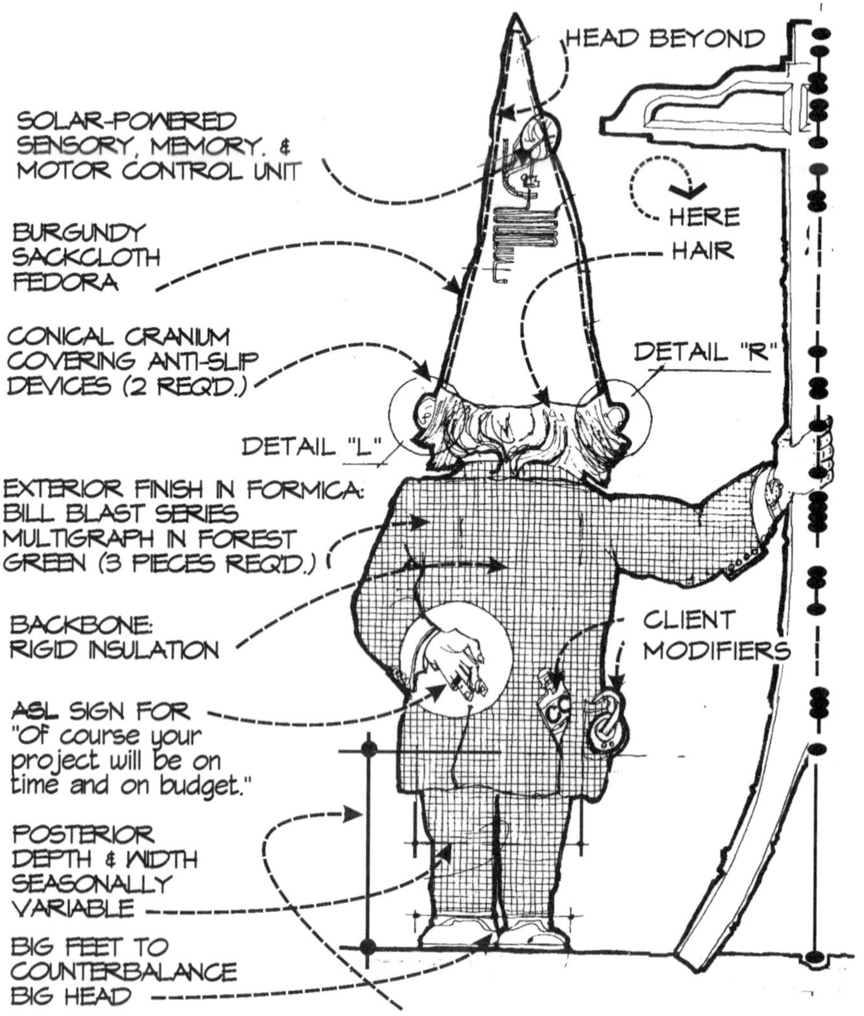

POSTERIOR ELEVATION ≈ 2

NOTE: Contractor shall make good all surfaces...& people

LIMITED WARRANTY: IF YOU PUT THIS DRAWING IN YOUR POCKET AND IT CATCHES FIRE, WE WILL REPLACE THE POCKET.

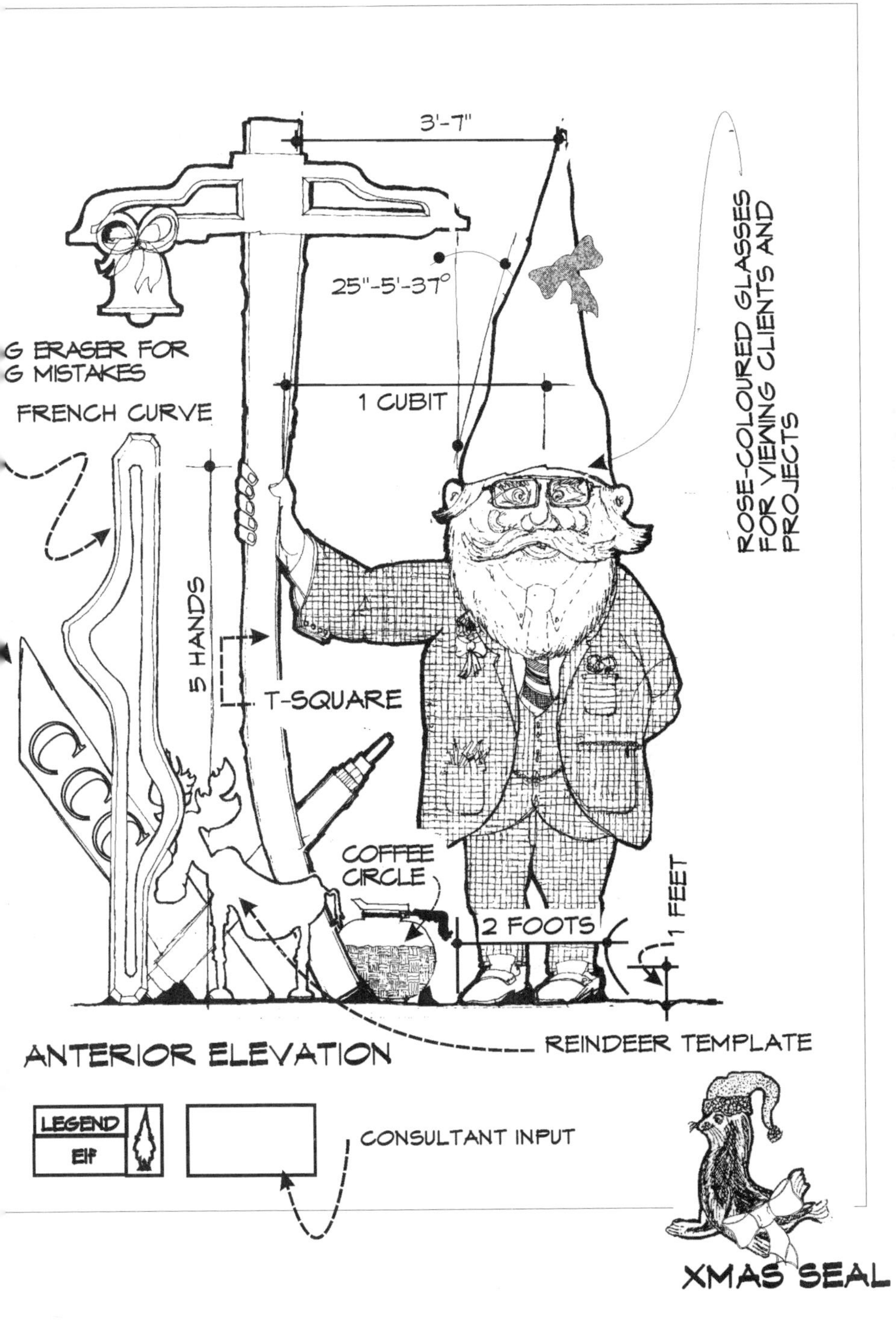
3'-7"
25"-5'-37°
ROSE-COLOURED GLASSES FOR VIEWING CLIENTS AND PROJECTS
G ERASER FOR
G MISTAKES
FRENCH CURVE
1 CUBIT
5 HANDS
T-SQUARE
COFFEE CIRCLE
2 FOOTS
1 FEET
ANTERIOR ELEVATION
REINDEER TEMPLATE
LEGEND
Elf
CONSULTANT INPUT
XMAS SEAL

TERRA TOY TOTER

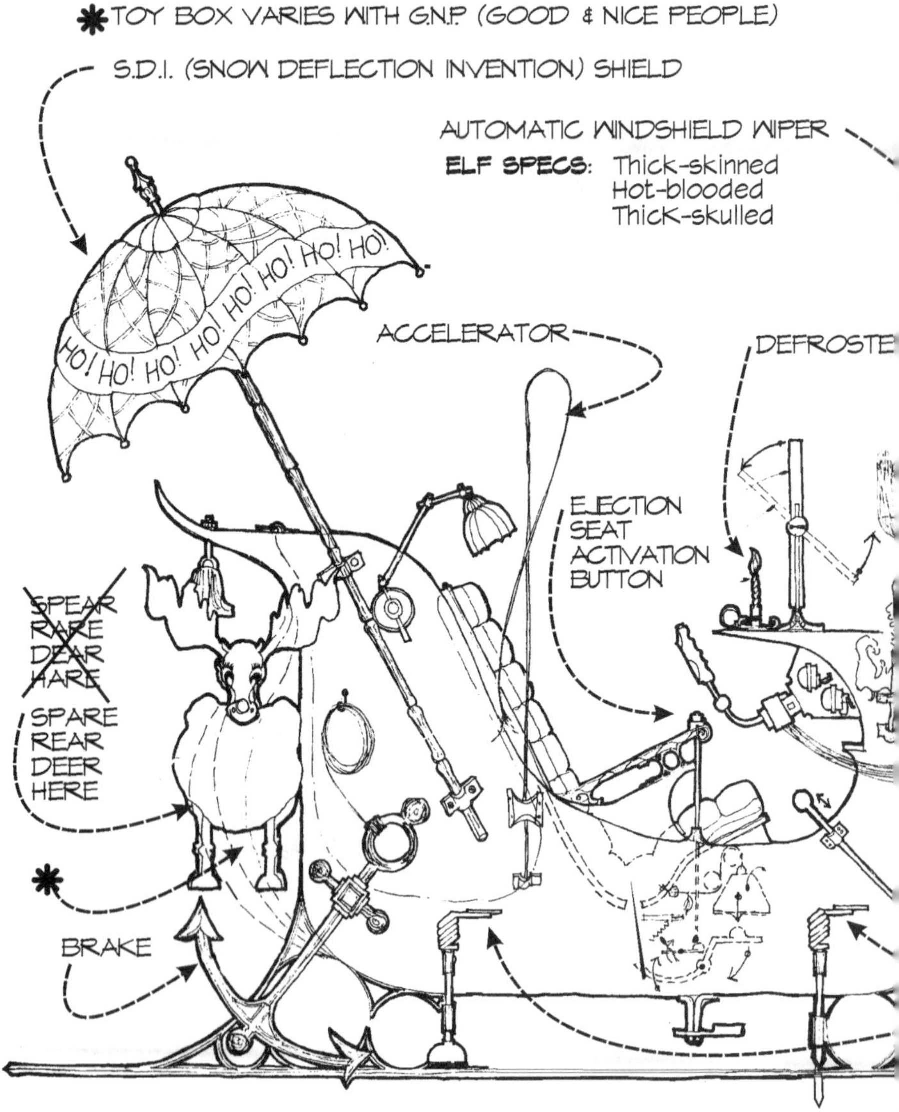

NOTE: QUALITY CONTROL IS CRITICAL. THIS IS NO FLY-BY-KNIGHT OPERATIC

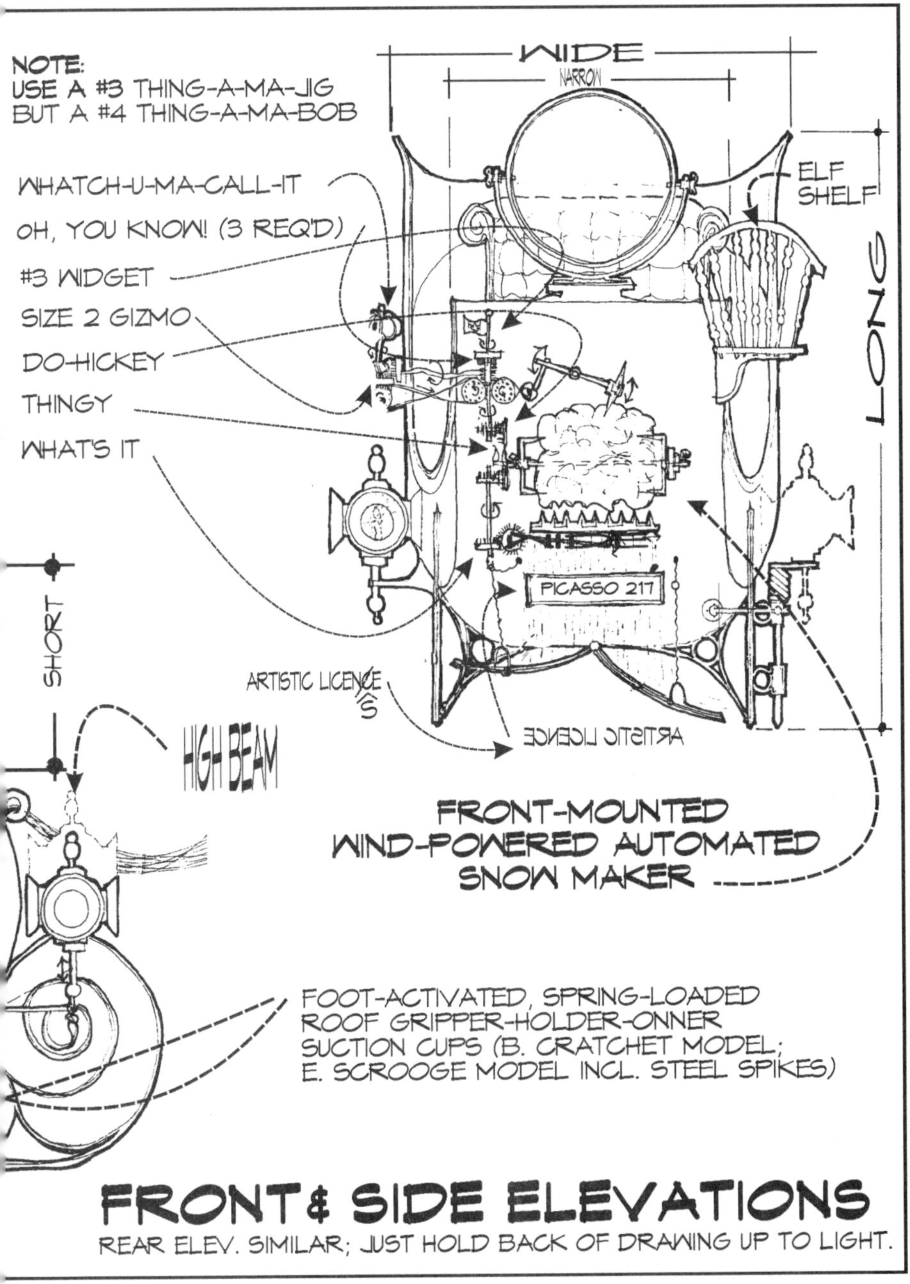

FRONT & SIDE ELEVATIONS

REAR ELEV. SIMILAR; JUST HOLD BACK OF DRAWING UP TO LIGHT.

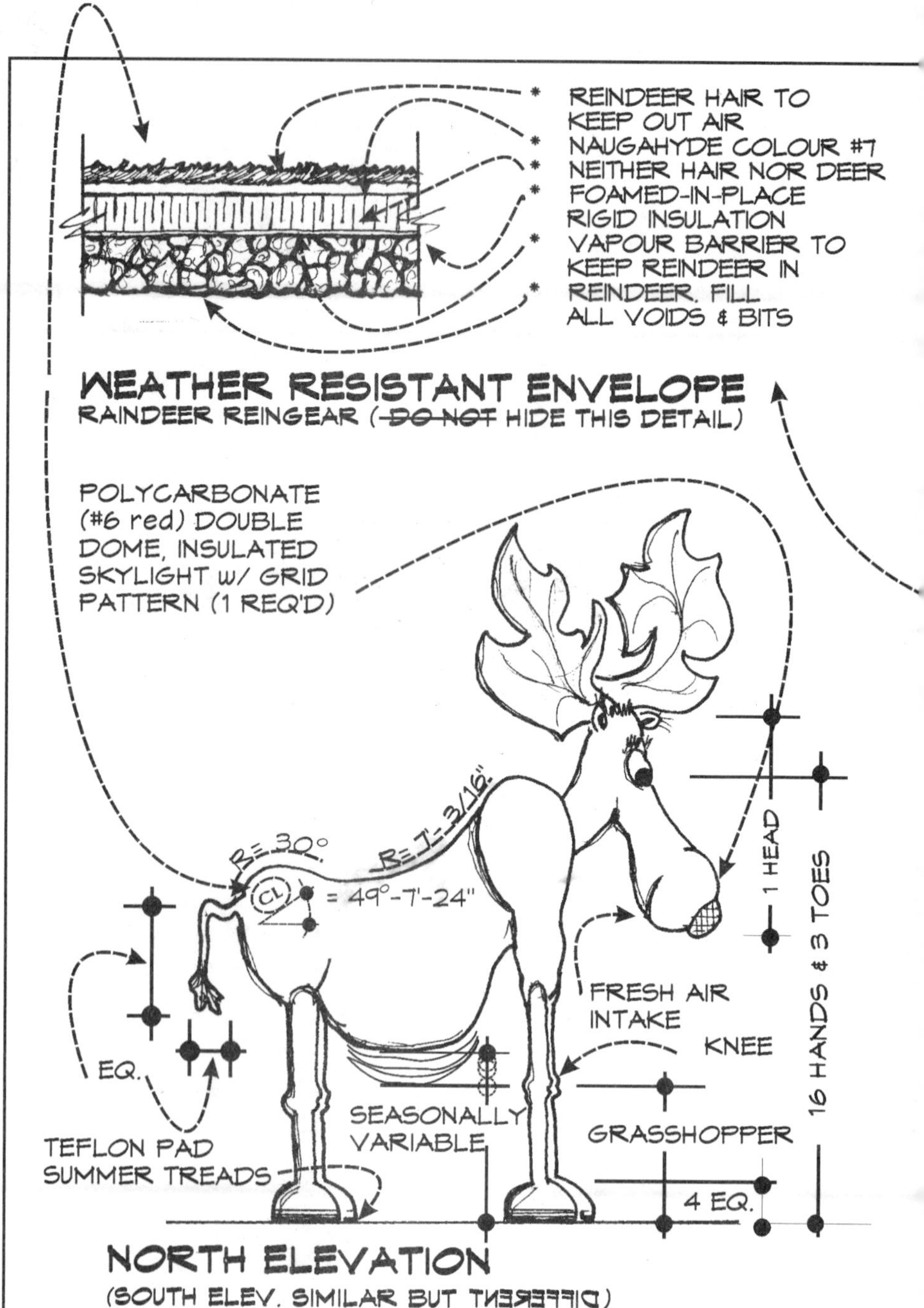
REINDEER HAIR TO KEEP OUT AIR
NAUGAHYDE COLOUR #7
NEITHER HAIR NOR DEER
FOAMED-IN-PLACE RIGID INSULATION
VAPOUR BARRIER TO KEEP REINDEER IN
REINDEER. FILL ALL VOIDS & BITS
WEATHER RESISTANT ENVELOPE
RAINDEER REINGEAR (~~DO NOT~~ HIDE THIS DETAIL)
POLYCARBONATE (#6 red) DOUBLE DOME, INSULATED SKYLIGHT w/ GRID PATTERN (1 REQ'D)
R= 30°
R= 7'-3/16"
CL
= 49°-7'-24"
1 HEAD
16 HANDS & 3 TOES
FRESH AIR INTAKE
KNEE
EQ.
GRASSHOPPER
SEASONALLY VARIABLE
TEFLON PAD SUMMER TREADS
4 EQ.
NORTH ELEVATION
(SOUTH ELEV. SIMILAR BUT TNƎЯƎFFID)

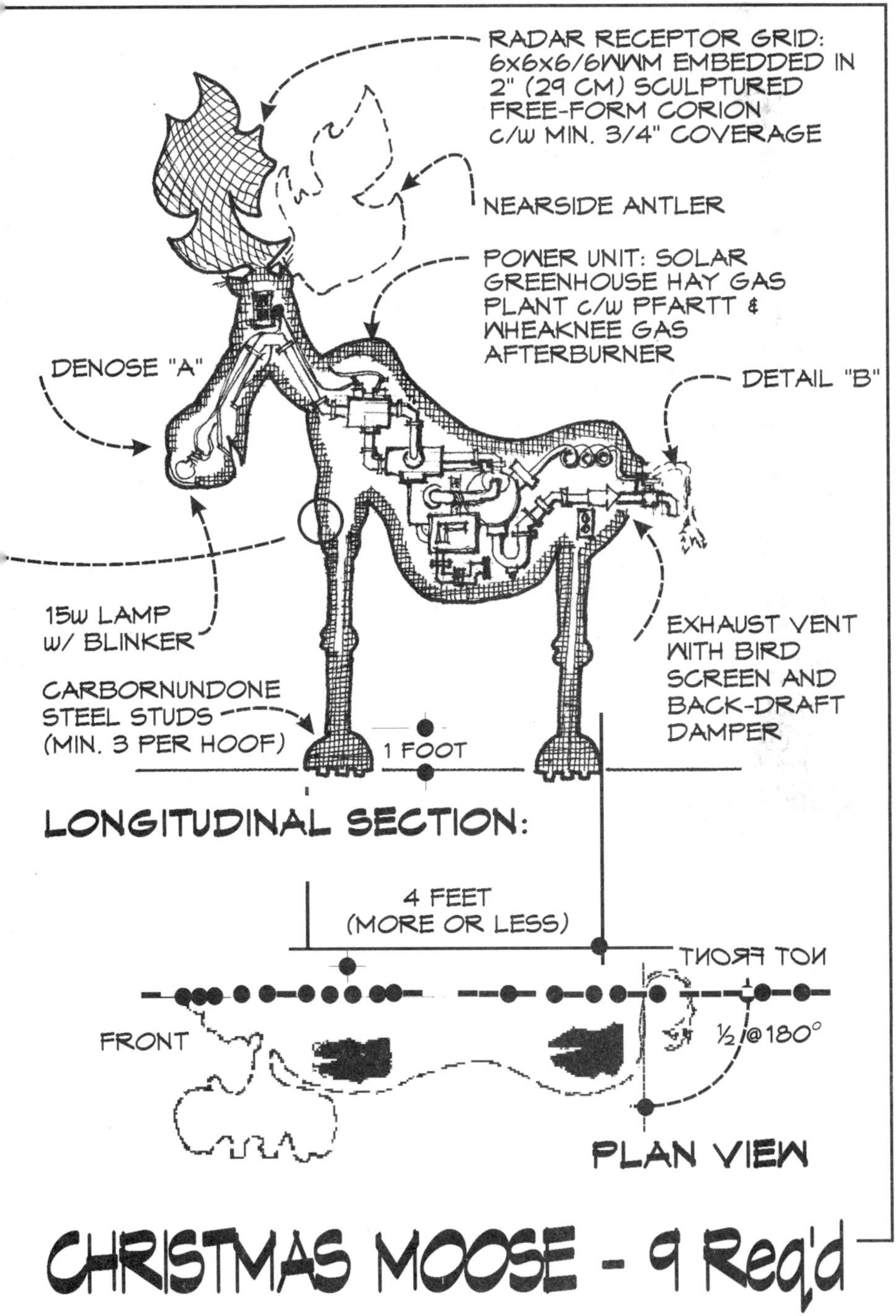

CHRISTMAS MOOSE - 9 Req'd

TANNENBAUM TORNADO

1 Drink and you want to pollinate;.
2 your needles drop off;
3 you feel like Paul Bunyan;
4 and you smell like Babe the blue ox.
5 TIMBERRRRRRRRRRRRRRRRRR!

3 oz. tequila
1 oz. creme de menthe
3 cherries
lice of slime

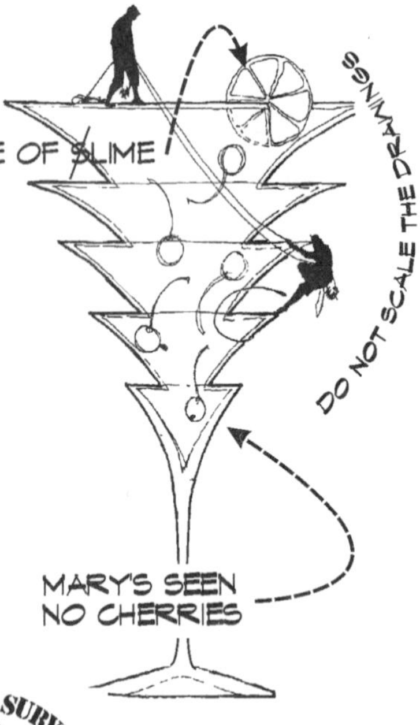

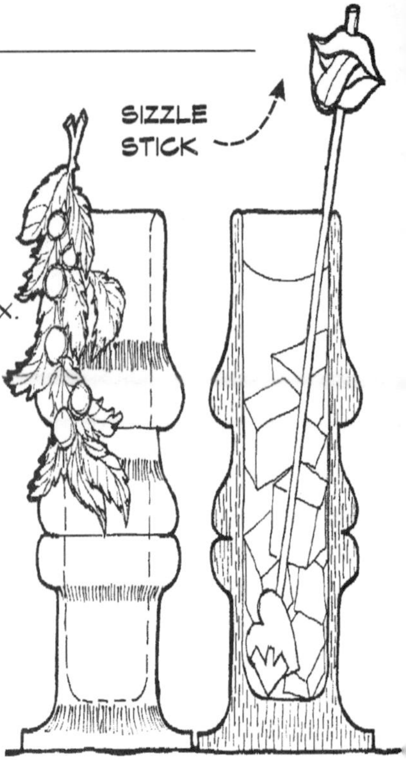

MISTLETOE MADNESS (a.k.a. MINT TWOLIPS)

Causes spontaneous puckering and makes you indescribably attractive.

Clip tips off 8 mint leaves & crush in sugar. Add 3 dashes of club soda & 1 dash of lemon juice. Plus 1 dash of aromatic bitters (opt.) and 2.5 oz. of bourbon. Chill in tall glass w/ crushed ice for 3 hrs. SERVE.

1/3 DOZ. GLASSES FROM "LARGE INTERESTING PERFECT SERIES"
"L.I.P.S" by BODI
A FOUR-BODING EXPERIENCE

STRIVE TO SURVIVE
DON'T DRINK & ~~DRIVE~~ FLY

ELF FUEL - DRINKS FOR DINKS

DRINKING TIPS:

1) 12%, 15%, & 27.89%

2) Always drink from the near side of the glass.

PUGILIST PUNCH

Non-Alcoholic: With this you get punch drunk!

2 cups strong tea
3/4 cups lemon juice
2 cups orange juice
1 cup sugar
2 tbs. lime juice
12 sprigs mint
Strain & add 8 slices of pineapple.
Add 5 pints of chilled ginger ale and club soda w/ crushed ice.

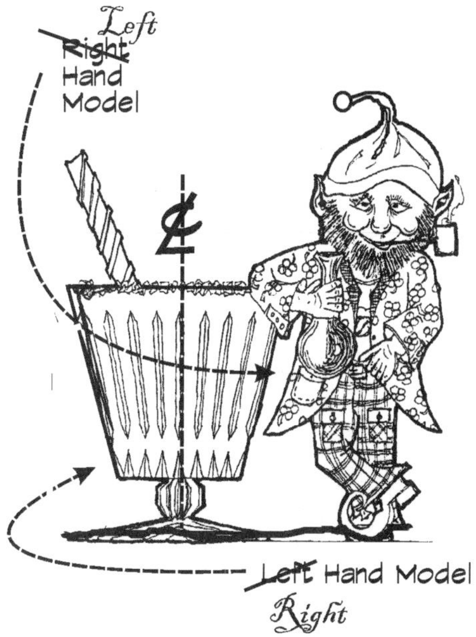

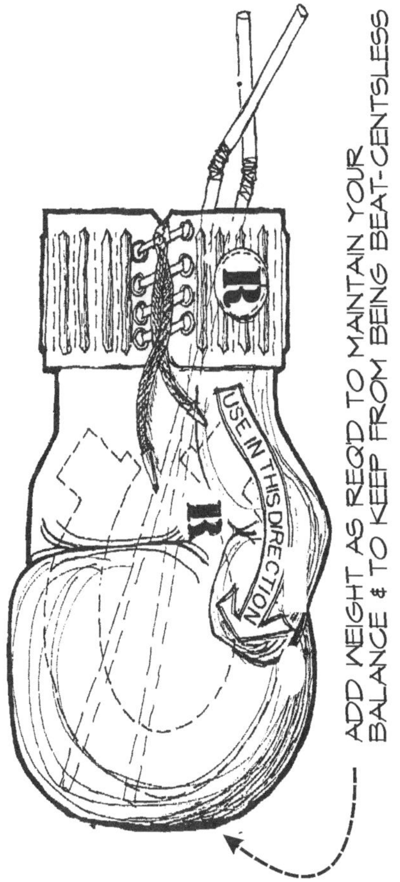

Chill glass & warm date.
Lime & sea salt rim.
2 oz. tequila
1 oz. sambuca
1 oz. lime juice & 1 ice cube
½ licorice stick - shove in

ELECTRIC ELF ELIXIR

Makes you as mischievous as the little people but with bigger ideas and the guts to try them out. Creates an insatiable desire to kiss short people and wear curly toed shoes.

3) Use less liquor if mixing drinks at your home.

4) At your brother-in-law's place pour it in.

TRANSPORTATION: MECHANICAL ORIGAMI SWANS PULLING RICKSHA

(YOKOZUNA) SUMO SANTA

a.k.a. SUOMI SANTA in Finland

EDITOR'S NOTE:
PEOPLE NEVER SEE SANTA BECAUSE HE DRESSES AND BEHAVES TO BLEND IN WITH THE LOCAL PARTY SCENE.

EXTERIOR SIDING CAN BE REMOVED WITH A BLOWTORCH OR WIRE WHEEL. THIS IS EASIER TO DO AFTER THE UPPER STOREY HAS BEEN REMOVED.
IF IN DOUBT, RE: WHAT TO REMOVE, JUST WING IT.
DELICATE RENOVATION WORK SHALL BE EXECUTED WITH THIS PRECISION INSTRUMENT.
REMOVE UPPER STOREY
SEE CRITICAL DETAIL #7 - IT'S HERE SOMEWHERE.
CUT ALONG DOTTED LIN
GUT INTERIOR: REMOVE ELEC. WIRING, HEATING, AND A/C UNIT
BEFORE
REMOVE LOWER 2 FEET OF FOUNDATION

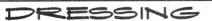

DRESSING

SAUTÉ ½ CUP ONIONS IN 12 tbs. BUTTER **+1** 2 CUPS OYSTERS (THEY TASTE BETTER WITHOUT THE SHELLS)

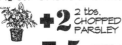

+2 2 tbs. CHOPPED PARSLEY **+3** 1½ tsp. salt, 4 tbs. capers, ½ tsp. paprika

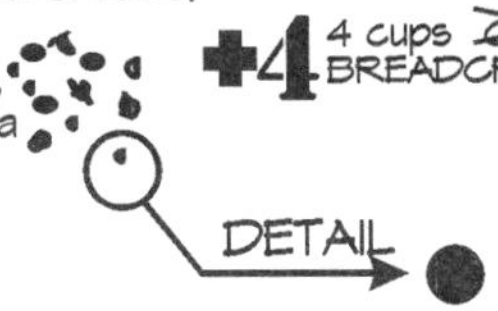

+4 4 cups ~~CRUMMY~~ BREADCRUMBS

= 5 CUPS DRESSING. (NOW GET STUFFED)

DURING

25min/lb @ 350°F - ROAST UNTIL YOUR GOOSE IS COOKED

✱ THESE EXPENSIVE & USELESS BOOTIES ARE NECESSARY TO PROVE THIS IS A CLASS ACT.

✱ IN THIS RENO, WE DON'T ADD A WING, WE REMOVE IT!

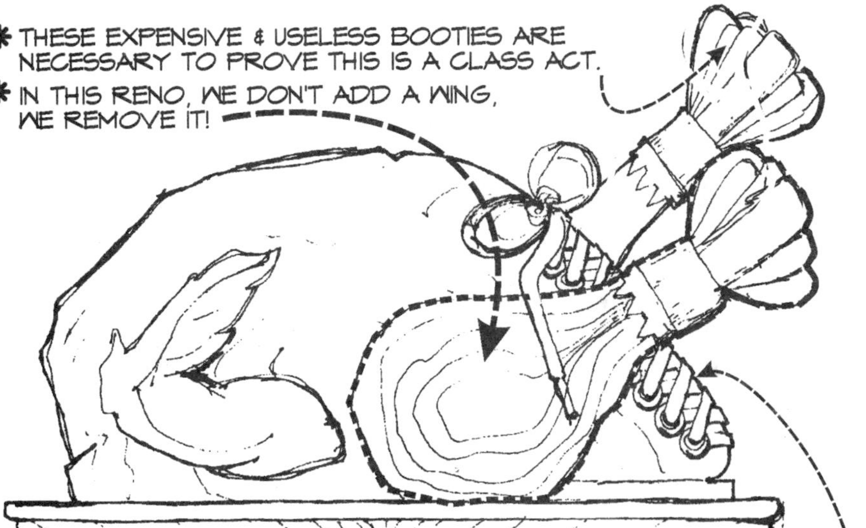

GIVE SOMEBODY YOU LOVE THE BIRD
(BUZZARD MAY BE SUBSTITUTED ONLY IN TORONTO)

& AFTER

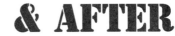

IT IS CONSIDERED IN POOR TASTE TO TIE UP TURKEY WITH OLD SKATE LACES (EVEN IN SASKATCHEWAN)

TURKEY RENOVATION

EDITOR'S NOTE #1
Although it is not considered one of the official How-To-Christmas documents, this page was found with them and was included for academic interest. Undeciphered since its discovery on an Upsala hearth in 937 A.D. (After Dusting), it is hoped that the document's true meaning may be discovered by paleoarchisociolinguiologists.

(Don't call us, we'll call you!)

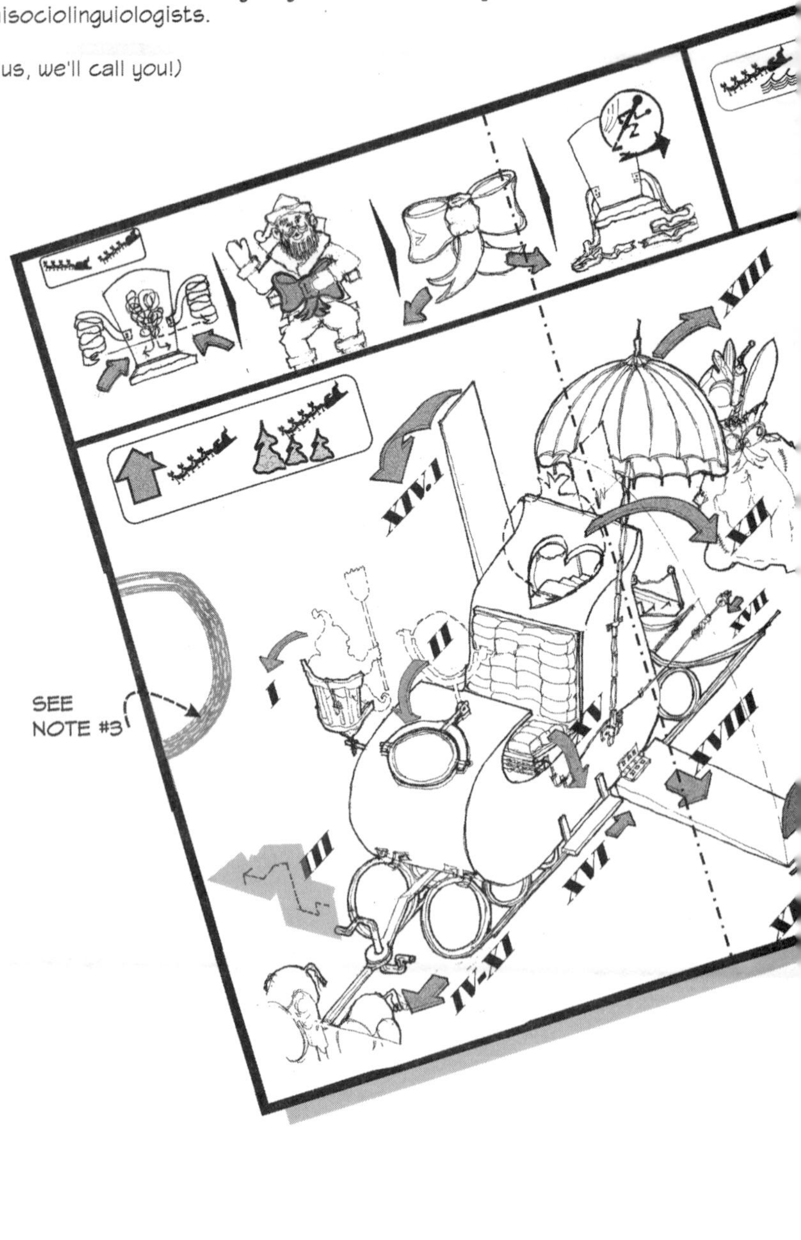

EDITOR'S NOTE #2

Of all the documents found, this was the only one printed on thicker parchment and appears to have been folded for convenience while travelling.

EDITOR'S NOTE #3

The document appears to have been subjected to extreme cold, and a mug stain was noted in the left upper quadrant. Chemical analysis indicates that it is a mixture of apple, cinnamon, nutmeg, mace, clove, allspice, egg, madeira, brandy, and a yellow polyethylene-butyl product.

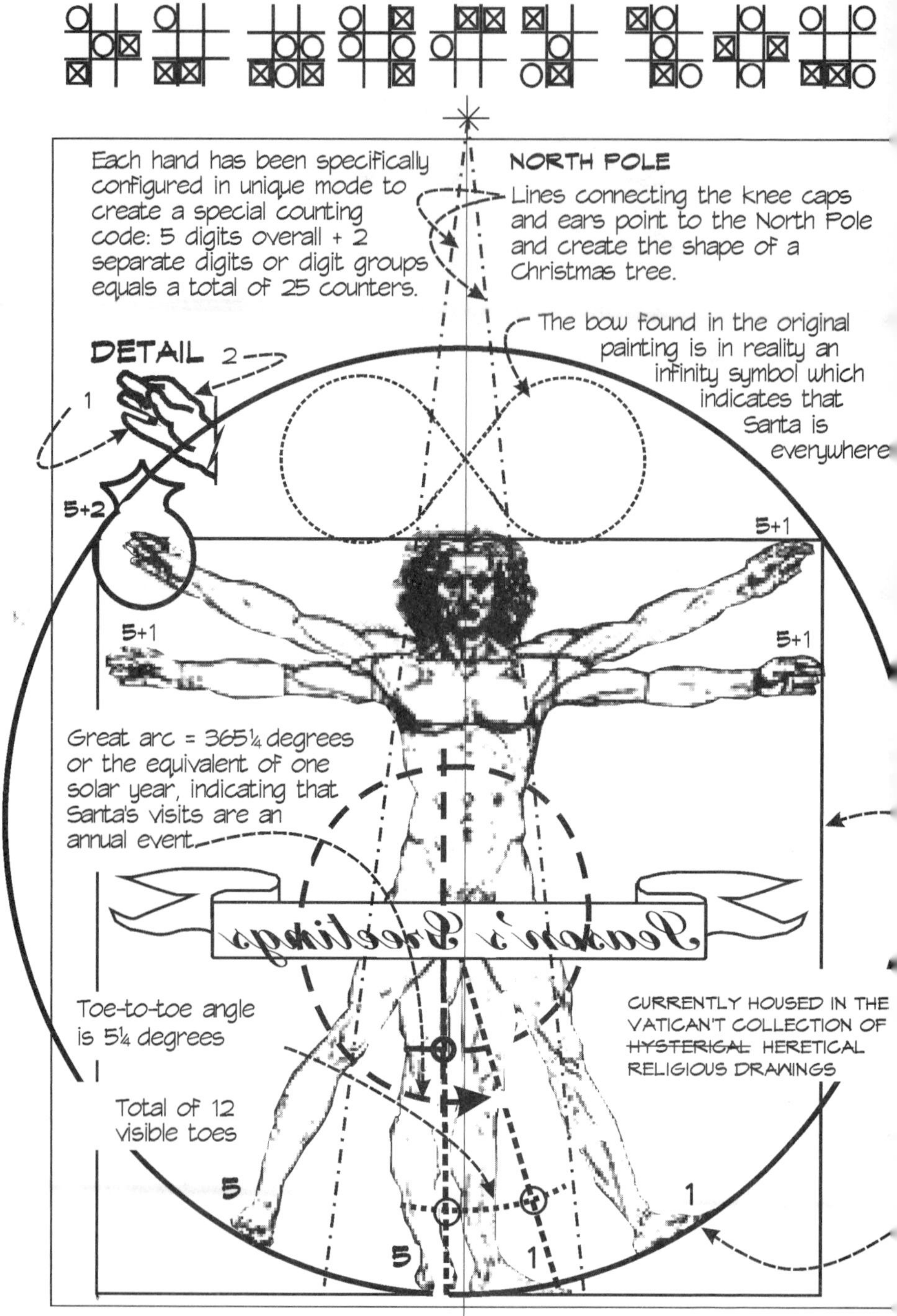

EDITOR'S NOTE: FOUND WITH SANTA'S WORKING DRAWINGS, THE PAINTING SHOWN ON THE RIGHT, AUTHENTICATED AS PAINTED BY *THE* DA VINCI, GRAND MASTER OF THE ELVES, PROVIDES VIEWERS WITH NUMEROUS CLUES PROVING HIS MEMBERSHIP IN THIS ANCIENT

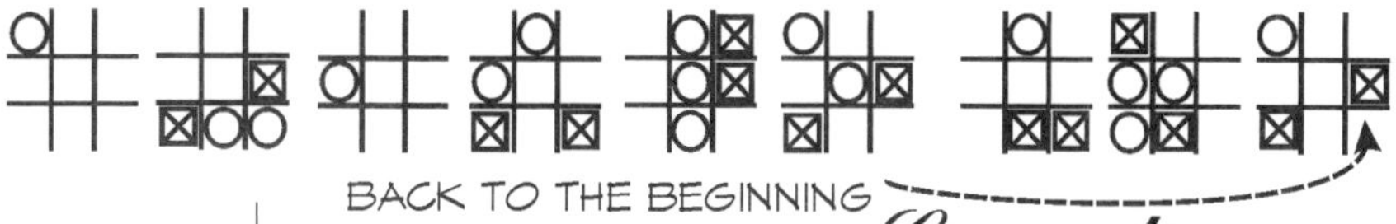

Connection

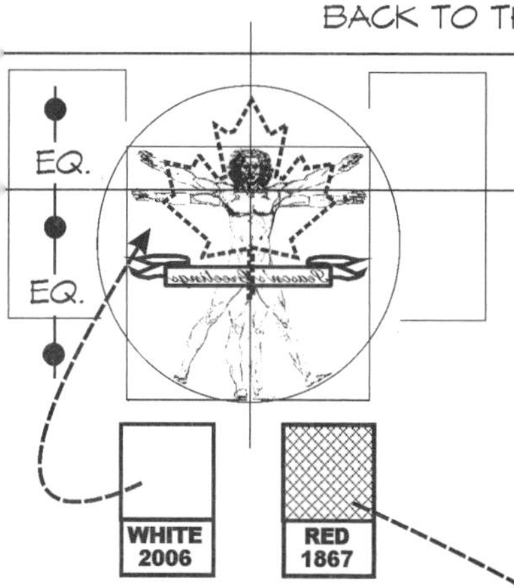

CANADIAN CONCOCTION

1) The Canadian flag sized and imposed on the da Vinci Claus shows that the maple leaf's main points match the positioning of the arms.

2) A geographic link is found in the name of Canada's most northerly city: TUKTOYAKTUK meaning "Place where toys are packaged for good children."

3) The colours of the Canadian flag match the colours of Santa's outfit.

SYMBOLISM

Painted by Leo in 1456, the original oil "Terra Santa Giftus" hung for years behind Santa's desk. Stolen, and subsequently hidden by Scrooge in 1844, it was replaced by this sketch which Leo redrew in 1923 while on vacation in Italy but which he accidentally left ona Roma streetcara.

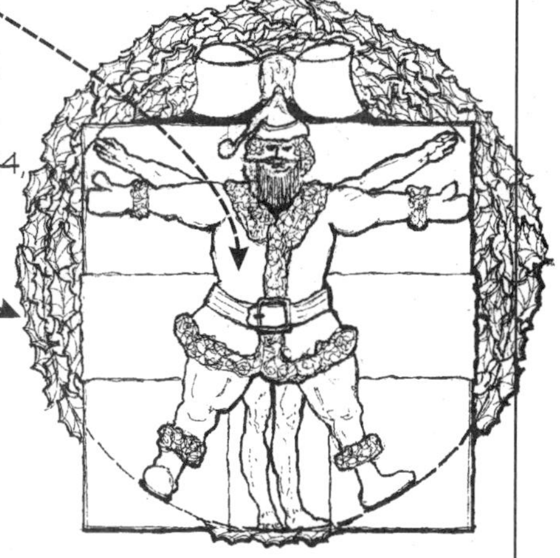

ORIGINAL PAINTING
(ACRYLIC ON POLYCARBONATE WITH FELT, FUR, LEAVES, & BERRIES)

The circle of the da Vinci Claus is representative of holly wreaths, igloos, snowballs, snowpersons, and the world where Santa spreads happiness.

The square represents presents and the box in which the D.I.Y. trees are delivered. Together they are the essence of the Santa Xmas.

The multi-armed form serves only to hide the secret of the da Vinci Claus, a code telling us that Santa visits every twenty-fifth (25) of December (12).

THE DA·VINCI CLAUS

GUILD, WHILE AT THE SAME TIME AFFIRMING THE LOCATION OF BOTH SANTA AND HIS WORKSHOP AND DEMONSTRATING THAT SANTA, THE NORTH POLE, AND XMAS ARE CANADIAN INVENTIONS.
(PATENT PENDING)

harmonica for the homeless

"Yeowk! Yeowk!" Ardie yowled in my face.

I jumped back before Ardie could throw any more soup on me. I shot a quick glance toward the chaplain's office and, with no Nelson in sight, rapped Ardie on the knuckles with my metal soup ladle, not hard enough to do any damage, but hard enough to let him know I meant business.

"Yeowk!" he whimpered, not in the bloodthirsty way he had roared a few seconds ago, but with the pain of a hurt kitten. "It's Christmas Eve, you bitch!" Then he whimpered some more. "That wasn't nice, Marylu," he said plaintively.

I felt lousy. For about two seconds. After all, Ardie had been terrorizing me for the past five and three-quarter months, and I had only recently found the gumption to smack back.

I was not the usual worker at the House of Hope (known as Hopeless House to those of us who had spent more than half an hour in the place). No, I was not a sweet do-gooder descending on the homeless and the disadvantaged as an angel of mercy, fuelled by an altruistic need to spread light to the needy. Nor was I an aspiring social worker aiming for enlightenment and hands-on experience with those cast aside by society.

None of the above. I was a shoplifter.

Let me explain.

I am not a criminal. In the weeks after Norman dumped me for the girl at the lotto booth (I wondered why he was buying so many tickets), I roamed aimlessly through the Bay, Holt Renfrew, Birks: all the stores that represented safety, tradition, and class. I looked at the jewellery, the perfume, the shoes, the scarves — the things that comforted me, as a consumer of note.

I had my own business as an event planner and knew the stores like the back of my nicely manicured hand. But somehow, one sweltering summer afternoon, when I thought of Norman and Tiffany in the mountains at the cool cabin that used to be mine, everything went black while I was in the handbags and accessories department. When I came to, I was walking through the parkade wearing $200 kid leather gloves. In the hottest summer in a decade.

The floorwalker thought it was hilarious. So did the judge. I got off easy. Ha ha. Six months of community service at the House of Hope, to teach me how the disadvantaged live and provide me with some incentive to appreciate all my blessings. Right.

So there I was, in Hopeless House, nearing the end of my six-month sentence to daily encounters with the filthy, the deranged, the helpless, the ranting, the roaring, the ripped-off segment of society that was looking for somebody to blame for their shattered, broken lives, and half the time, it seemed as if I — the innocent (sort of) person at the other end of the ladle — was handy.

Nelson told me not to take it personally. Well, excuse me. Nelson is six feet tall, balding, an ex-biker turned chaplain who could look at a kook like Ardie and silence him in a moment. But the minute Nelson returned to his office, Ardie would throw hot soup on me again. It was really hard to be an angel under these circumstances. If a nice stay in a jail cell with heroin addicts for best friends hadn't been the alternative, I would have thrown my soup ladle through Nelson's door and stampeded away months before. But it was a viciously icy Christmas Eve, and I had seven days to go.

Seven days and I would be free.

Free of the crowding, the smell, the claustrophobia, and, above all, the unrelenting noise. I tried not to let it get to me, but it was heartbreaking. Sure, I'd read all those articles about how public service and self-sacrifice are enriching and rewarding. When I started my community service, I had fleeting moments of optimism, wild thoughts that maybe I had been sent there for a reason, and eventually when I "graduated," I would receive a glowing tribute, a major award, perhaps an endowment for being a good person (despite the

$200 gloves and that really nasty episode in court), and then I would be as close to a saint as any mortal could be.

But by the time my sentence was almost at an end, I no longer aspired to sainthood. After five months of Ardie and the soup throwing (even though Nelson told him sternly not to abuse the workers); of seeing Liz, one of the regulars, stagger in every evening drunk and vile, with eyes that never focused, and knowing that her day must have contained indignities I could never imagine nor want to; of having a 14-year-old girl offer me favours for a pack of cigarettes (I don't even smoke, for Pete's sake); of listening to Wild Man rant about the evils done to him by the world (Nelson had to disarm him at least five times in as many months, and yet he never turned him away), I no longer had faith.

Faith, in my opinion, is determined by a belief that the world is good. That people are good. And that we have the power to change the destiny of others by good deeds. That our own lives can be changed by chance and illuminating circumstance. I could not believe in this abstract notion of faith when, daily, I encountered people humiliated by life, either by their own inability to move on or by society's abdication of responsibility to help them do so.

I saw Nelson helming Hopeless House — kind, strong, tough — but I also saw his frustration and powerlessness in the face of reduced civic funding and the daily battles with violence and despair. With my experience pitching and pleading as a public relations gal and event planner, I knew

I could show him how to get through to the head honchos in the City, but, here, I was an outsider.

I was realistic about my place in that madhouse. I was not a mover and a shaker. I was not Mother Teresa. I was not Florence Nightingale. I was not even my best me. I was somebody marking time, serving soup, wiping down the tables, doing my best not to have to clean the washrooms (although sometimes I couldn't avoid it, no matter how many times I said I had a really bad stomach ache), and trying to get the hell out of there. I didn't have the backbone or the spirit for that.

Seven days. Just seven days. And I would be free. I would be back in the world of pedicures and bistros and shoe sales and art galleries, and I would never have to think about all that again.

We had started serving turkey dinner at noon in two-hour shifts. Most volunteers worked one or two shifts. I had been there since noon, and it was after 6 p.m. Already I had ladled soup and plunked plates of turkey and fixings in front of my share of a thousand "guests." I was always bemused by that quaint title for the throngs that descended on Hopeless House, but then I, shoplifter extraordinaire, was dubbed a "host." So I guess it made some sort of sense.

Outside, it was –30°C. Inside, the atmosphere was even grimmer than usual. Our last shift.

At six o'clock, I had rapped on Nelson's door.

"Yes?" He had looked up from what I knew were the donation projections for the next year, not even seeing me for a moment. He seemed sadder than I had known him to be, even though, generally speaking, I had trouble attributing finer emotions to anybody with tattoos.

"It looks as if it's going to be a rough night," I said with the reluctantly gained experience of a woman who had lived through Wild Man's rampage on Halloween, when he had broken five chairs and the jaw of one volunteer. In November, I had found Liz lying on the step outside in –25°C weather and dragged her in, even though she had kicked me in the back when I turned to open the door. I wasn't up to much more, and I knew it.

Seven days.

There was going to be trouble. I could tell from the noise level and from something in the air. Popular opinion holds that the homeless should be grateful for every crumb, and most of them are. Reg, an impossibly scrawny guy who says he was a geologist before he became a Dumpster diver, is impeccably courteous and appreciative. Most, when they take their meals from you, are quietly thankful. But sometimes, underneath, there is a current of rage. How did this happen to them? Why aren't they somewhere in a warm house with a family and a TV, instead of in a huge, barking room of noise and anguish?

I would feel the same way. I would want to howl at the moon, "I make a mean martini. I know Robert's Rules of Order. I can read a budget. How did I end up here?" And, of course, at the back of my mind, was always "What would it take for me to be here? How did they get here? And how can I feel superior, when maybe, with a few twists of fate, it could happen to me?"

When I got into those uncharacteristically contemplative moments, Nelson always reminded me that we were there to provide some joy and dignity to our clients, whatever their circumstances. "Marylu," he would say quietly, "we are here for the unlovely." Just like Nelson. Whenever I complained, he came up with some line that stopped me in my tracks. Strange guy. But then, Nelson was sort of isolated in his own way. I think he was every bit as lonely as any of our clients. "Our" clients. That was a slip of the tongue. Because I'd be free in seven days. Seven days.

But that night, I was nervous. Really nervous. It wasn't just Ardie — he threw soup on me all the time. It was the way the Sledge looked at me. And Liz. It was Christmas Eve, and they were mad that nobody cared. Well, I cared. Sort of. I was serving soup, wasn't I?

Leona, one of the really saintly volunteers, looked at me from across the room, and I could see the strained look in her eyes. She was nervous, too. We had the usual dozen volunteers on that shift, but we were short on staff. Mike, our bouncer of choice, had been sent home with the flu. Nelson, three others, and Martin, the chef, were in charge.

At the far end of the room, a drunk staggered around. He sent a soup bowl and a glass crashing to the floor, and the noise increased the tension.

Nelson came out of his office, walked over to the drunk, and hauled him to the door. I saw him talking to him really intensely. He even grabbed him by the shoulders and shook him. That's when I knew the night was going bad. Because no matter how stressful things got, we could always count on Nelson to be kind and gentle and never lose patience with the clients.

I was getting a bad feeling. Maybe it was that I was nervous about Wild Man and Ardie and a few of the more violent guys. But mostly it was that it was Christmas Eve and nothing was very Christmassy in Hopeless House. I saw a few smiling faces, but mostly there was a feeling of despair and anger. I sure didn't want anybody to take it out on me. I was sorry I had ever laid eyes (or hands) on those damned gloves.

I walked back to the kitchen. My hands were wet with nervous perspiration. I wiped them on my apron, or I knew I would never be able to lift the coffee pots.

"Marylu, are you all right?" asked Martin, who had worked at a five-star hotel until drinking took him on a downward ride that landed him sober and working at Hopeless House.

"Fine," I said, thinking, *just seven more days, seven more days.*

I glanced toward the entrance. Nelson was back in his office. The drunk had settled down and returned to his seat.

There was somebody else at the door. A newcomer.

He was a tiny man, well into his 70s, wearing a coat that

was too threadbare for that frigid evening.

Great, another one. I snapped at him, "Dinner started at six."

He looked at me through thick glasses that revealed remarkably green eyes. Surprising, as the rest of him was faded. Faded coat. Faded white hair. Faded fedora squashed on top. Fragile skin lined with wrinkles. Frail little faded hands. Faded little black shoes. Nondescript.

I felt ashamed, although he did nothing but look at me. He moved as if to leave. I felt a pang of something unfamiliar. I think it might have been guilt. "We'll find you a place. Come with me."

After some negotiating, I found him a place beside Liz and went to get him a plate.

He'll be sorry, I thought. The way the night was going, we would all be lucky to escape without injury. In my heart, I wanted to run to the door and hurl myself home, all the way home, and never go back.

I looked at the door, yearning for freedom. But the thought of a jail cell held me there, coffee pot in hand. And a look at Leona and Nelson, who were stalwartly moving among the throng. Leona found a bowl of soup for the newcomer, who thanked her quietly. He ate quickly and — strange to say — sweetly, seeming to savour every mouthful.

On the far side of the hall, two men started to rap their bowls on the table. Soon, the men beside them started to rap their bowls, too. The din was excruciating. I looked at Nelson.

To my dismay, he didn't seem to know what to do. There was anger in the room, and although it had nothing to do with us, it was terrifying.

Nelson walked over to them, but they ignored him. They were big guys, and there were three, no five, no seven of them, just hitting the table with their bowls. The rest of the room seemed undecided on whether to join in or hide under the tables.

Another noise started to wheedle through the air, fighting the din. I couldn't take the banging chorus from the drunks anymore. My eardrums were roaring. I had to do something. The banging was making me shake with terror and rage.

For a person who has trouble lifting a bag of groceries without putting her back out, I was amazing. I grabbed a big metal garbage can, loaded as it was, and slammed it onto the floor as hard as I could. The sudden clang shocked everyone into silence. There was a startled moment. And in that moment, the sound was distinct.

A harmonica. And it was playing "Silent Night."

We all looked. It was the little guy, the latecomer. He was standing by his place, and he was playing "Silent Night" on an old harmonica.

The whole room just stopped. I swear. It was as if we were frozen. The first few phrases and everybody stopped what they were doing. Nelson was leaning over one of the bowl-banging guys — I can still see him, his muscles clenched, his hands on the table, and his head turned toward the music. And I can still see the bowl-banging guys, especially Big Ed. He was holding his bowl, absolutely still. Beside him, his pal was the same, staring at the old guy with the harmonica.

I looked around the rest of the room. At every table, people sat perfectly still, listening. Even Liz.

It wasn't just that the little guy could wheeze the notes out of the harmonica. He played that harmonica as if it were a violin, cello, trumpet, and oboe all rolled into one. And, especially, it was the feeling he put into it.

"Silent night, holy night ..." I had heard that song so many times in my life, from Perry Como to reggae, that it had ceased to have any meaning for me. But when he played it, it was as if I were hearing it for the first time. It was so pure, so strong, and so heartfelt. I felt as if I were surrounded by prayer.

Wow, this is wonderful, I thought. Then I realized that tears were running down my face.

I looked around the room. Liz was still staring straight ahead, but now a tear was gently trailing down her face. Ardie was just sitting, listening. Mad Man was totally still, and — no! Was that a tear in his eye? The look on Nelson's face broke my heart. It was as if we were all caught in a time warp, where nothing existed except "Silent Night" on the harmonica.

The old guy came to the end of it with "Sleep in heavenly peace, sleep in heavenly peace."

He paused, delicately wiped his mouth with a handkerchief, and slowly put his harmonica into an inner pocket in his coat. The room was absolutely still. A strange, magical stillness.

Then we all applauded, very formally, as if we were at Roy Thomson Hall. The musician bowed, with great dignity, to the north, east, south, and west of the room. He didn't say a word.

Then he carefully walked to the door. He seemed so frail — I didn't want him to go out into the night alone. I followed him.

"We have beds for the night," I said.

"I know."

"That was beautiful," I whispered inadequately.

He gave another little bow, pushed open the door, and walked off into the icy night.

Like an idiot, I stood there, staring at the door, wondering where he would sleep and who he was.

When I turned back to the room, it was ... different. Not that all of sudden people had manners like the queen or were hugging each other. But it seemed more peaceful. Ardie actually cleared his plate and cutlery and helped Leona with her tray of dishes. Liz was smiling. It was the first time I had seen her smile. And Nelson was ... Well, Nelson didn't look very good. I rushed over to him.

His eyes were moist. "Why can't it always be like this?" he said, looking around the room.

"Maybe we need to remember that it *can* be like this.

Maybe we always need to remember the little man with the harmonica."

Nelson looked at me. "What's with the 'we' business? Aren't you always saying you're out of here at the end of the month?"

I thought about that. And I thought about the little man with the harmonica. And then I heard these words come out of my mouth: "Maybe I could hang around for a week or two and help you with fundraising."

That was six years ago.

I still work at the House of Hope, and every Christmas Eve, I look for the little man with the harmonica. But he's never come back.

I worry about him, wonder how he is. Has he lasted all those winters? Did he fall into a final sleep in an alley? Or is he somewhere out there, playing the harmonica to another audience?

one dead turkey

The doorbell rang. I threw down my oven mitts and limped (dang those cheap slippers from the discount store) to the doorbell. I swung forced it open — reminding myself that a new lock was on my wish list the agenda — expecting to see a friendly face, in fact, maybe even a loving one. It was Christmas Day, after all, and I, in a some demented moment, had invited a small group of friends to dinner.

Instead, a dead turkey, hanging from the door frame, smacked me in the face. Yuck. I lurched back, jumping into one of the karate poses I had learned 20 years ago in acting class. No dead turkey was going to get the better of me.

In a few seconds, I realized that, right, it was just the turkey and me. And it wasn't really going to do much, except give me salmonella if I ate it. I shivered in the cold wind that blew past the turkey into my house.

I wiped my face with my sweater (which I wore every

Christmas to please my ancient third cousin Lillian, who had knit it for me in her hit-and-miss, semi-knotted style) and took a hard look at this turkey. It had no personality, nothing to distinguish it from other turkeys. It wasn't even cooked. It looked as if it had been hauled out of its meat department wrapping five minutes earlier.

I hadn't thought to look around for the delivery person. I hadn't noticed anybody running away. No point in looking for footsteps. Snow was drifting lightly onto the lane, shifting every second. At five in the afternoon, the sky had dimmed and the falling snow was the only light. Besides, who on earth would trek out here to put a turkey in my doorway? I lived in a small house on the outskirts of town, on heavily wooded land between two freeways.

Given my dramatic training, my mind whizzed through several scenarios: the turkey was a hostess gift, perhaps well intended but unfortunately presented. I thought about that for two and a half seconds and decided nobody sane would hang a dead turkey from a door and let it smack me in the face.

Next option: the turkey was a message from the gods. *Don't take that gig with the dinner theatre in Wisconsin. You will be served up in the reviews like this turkey.* I sort of agreed with that interpretation, as I had decided to turn this gig down, mostly because they were offering scale with no perks and the director was known for sending the cast to the hospital in hysterics.

It was during this cheery thought process that I noticed the note taped to the turkey: "You're next, Wanda."

Next? Next?? I looked up at the turkey. Although I had a much better figure, I sure didn't like the idea of hanging undressed in a doorway. It had to be a stupid joke.

I slammed the door on the turkey. Maybe it would go away. Maybe I had imagined it. Whatever, I didn't have time to deal with it. I had a dinner to prepare, and the other, real, respectable turkey that I had shoved into the oven needed basting, or at least some hopeful encouragement, and if that didn't work, some old-fashioned cursing.

I was sick and tired of Christmas dinners with groups of friends in restaurants, where you tried to be maniacally cheery over the plastic turkey and overworked waiters. This year would be different. It would be a nice, homey Christmas dinner, cooked by yours truly. And a dead turkey hanging in the doorway was not going to dampen my spirits one bit.

I had invited a small but vibrant group of eight:

- Dolores (my agent) and her Pekinese (the inevitable and dreaded Meow Meow)
- Gil (my lawyer)
- his wife, Nancy (a textile artist who specializes in Peruvian Noir)
- Serena (my best friend, who, even though she had just landed the Chicken Little commercial that I thought *I* had aced, was still brooding over

my two-day gig in a futuristic TV series. How was I to know she had been promised the role? Turns out they decided they wanted a tiny cute brunette — that's me — not a tall sexy blonde — that's Serena.)

- Michael (my ex-lover but mostly drunken mooch)
- Lillian (my elderly third cousin twice removed)
- Bajan (my holistic bartender/massage therapist)
- Arnie (my high school boyfriend turned handyman)

I was sort of bummed out because Brad, my new deadly dull boyfriend who was a guitarist with the Horrible Honeys, had cancelled after a blowup last week at the Laurier Lounge. I had told him he had absolutely no sense of humour. (Which is true.) After we exchanged a few colourful words about our relationship, he walked out in a huff, leaving me with the tab.

Despite that inconvenient setback, I was determined to make this dinner work. Peeking into the oven at the turkey, the yams, and the pre-mashed potatoes (okay, I cheated), I was not encouraged. Culinary skills were not on my résumé, a guilty secret I tried to keep to myself, as one of my major gigs had been as the spokesperson for Pretty Pantry frozen foods. To this day, people stop me on the street and ask for recipes. I usually run in the opposite direction, shouting, "So sorry! Daycare! It's a bitch!" Which is totally untrue and, anyway, I am beginning to border on being long in the tooth for needing daycare, but so what. I am justified in trying not to disillusion people on the great wisdom of the Pretty Pantry lady.

I scooped up some juice with the plastic spoon I had bought at the dollar store just for this occasion and poured it in the general direction of the turkey, comforting myself with the thought that everybody says basting is good.

The doorbell rang.

If it was that turkey again, there was going to be trouble.

I opened the door and leaped back, just in case. The turkey was still there. Behind it was Dolores, dressed in magenta.

Dolores was my lifeline to employment, which was why I had invited her and Meow Meow, even if Meow Meow loved to chew on my shoes. And the cute little thing always chose the most expensive ones, no matter how well I hid them. The one pair of Jimmy Choos I owned — garbage after my Halloween party. The Peter Fox platforms — history after Thanksgiving. Just give me five minutes alone with that Pekinese and she would never chew a Choo again.

Dolores was very dramatic, with her black kohled eyes and wild wardrobe that always crossed several eras and style lines. I was never sure what colour her hair was going to be. Maybe this is why she hadn't been getting me many gigs lately. Probably none of the ad agencies or casting directors recognized her in meetings. Her hair today stuck out in magenta spikes, some of which were turning lavender with the dusting of snow on the points. Even Meow Meow was dyed magenta. (I thought about reporting Dolores to some animal abuse organization but remembered that she used only vegetable dyes. Besides, Meow Meow and I weren't exactly best friends. I didn't care what colour she was as long as she stayed away from me and my shoes.)

"Did you see anybody on the road?" I asked.

Dolores peered at me over her dark purple-framed glasses. "Well, hello, how are you, Dolores? Merry Christmas. Have a good trip over the damned potholed roads that lead to this godforsaken dump?"

I pointed at the turkey. "Somebody left that for me."

"How sweeeeeet," she sang in her smoker's baritone. "Another turkey for Christmas."

"Look at the note," I said.

She ducked under the turkey and glanced at the note from beside me. "Damn. You should never have turned down that show at the Beacon."

"Nobody sends hate notes over rejections."

Snow swirled past us. She slammed the door shut.

"Then maybe it's Michael. You know he's a wild card."

"Michael can barely afford a six pack. He's not going to spring for a 20-pound turkey."

"Is Serena still cheesed off about *Bad Ballroom on Mercury?*"

"The series was cancelled after three episodes. She should get over it. Plus, she got Chicken Little."

"Career death," pronounced Dolores. (Serena was represented by Dolores's arch rival, Howie Lamont.)

She opened the door again and viewed the turkey, hanging like a fat, greasy hunk of mistletoe. I guess it reminded her of somebody because the next thing she said was "How about Arnie? Is he still mooning over you?"

"That was 20 years ago! He should get a life!"

"Hmm," said Dolores. "Still have the stalker?"

"It was never a stalker," I said firmly. "Just some crazy notes, and nothing has happened in months ..." I looked up at the turkey and the note. Damn. I wish I had never taken that sultry role in the low-budget thriller. Only about three people saw it, but, lucky me, one of them sent me weird love notes for a year.

"Any news on the sexual harassment case?" She shut the door again, shifted Meow Meow to the other arm, and trailed snow into the foyer.

A few months ago, I had reported Dez Dirk, a low-budget producer, to the union when his hand had rested on certain of my body parts during a callback. It was embarrassing. I am too old for such nonsense. Maybe that's why I had the gumption to lodge a complaint. Younger women are often too afraid of retaliation in the form of blacklisting. But the case was dragging on, and I had received several nasty letters from his lawyer and one obscene phone call.

I was getting depressed over the long list of suspects. Anybody could have left the turkey. On the other hand,

Dolores and I tended to go overboard when we were riffing together, and it was likely that we were just blowing smoke to satisfy our wild imaginations.

Dolores set Meow Meow on the floor. I had hidden all my shoes in an upstairs closet, so I was able to bare my teeth at the purple pet from hell.

"Hello, cutie! Merry Christmas."

"She knows you're lying," said Dolores.

Meow Meow made a beeline to my feet and attached herself to one of my slippers, shaking her cute frilly little ears and cute little magenta ribbon, while digging her cute little teeth into my bunion (acquired during a tour of *Chorus Line*).

The door blew open. I stifled my groan of pain and slammed the door on the annoying turkey, narrowly missing Meow Meow's little magenta tail (darn!), but at least the noise startled her enough that she let go and roamed around the room, finally settling in front of the faux fireplace.

"So who do you think left the turkey?" asked Dolores, kicking off her shoes and falling into my lumpy armchair. She helped herself to the pitcher of martinis I had left on the coffee table next to a bowl of decorative glass marbles. When she picked up the pitcher, a slip of paper drifted to floor. What was that? An old grocery list? I leaned over to pick it up, but Dolores grabbed it first. She loved to snoop.

She squinted and read, "'Remember *And Then There Were None?* You're the first, Wanda.'"

I spluttered, "Where did *that* come from? What is this? Agatha Christie crazy time? And am I next or first? Am I playing second banana to a turkey?"

I knew I wasn't making much sense, but this second note rattled me.

Dolores poured her martini and frowned.

"How many people know you're throwing a Christmas Day soirée?"

"Nobody," I said, scowling at Meow Meow, who was eyeing my slippers again. "Only the people I invited. You know how I am about privacy." (This has been an issue between Dolores and me for years. She says I need to make myself available to my fans. I say "What fans?" If I had fans, I would be famous, and if I were famous, surely I would be rich. In the meantime, I want to feel anonymous and safe at the grocery store and in my own home.)

"So if only the people you invited know you're having company for dinner ..."

I didn't like where she was going with this. If Dolores was right, one of the guests-to-be had decorated my doorway with the turkey and left the note under the martini pitcher. I'd put the pitcher there half an hour ago. Suddenly I felt a chill move from my neck down to my heels. Somebody had been in the house.

What had I done after making the martinis? Gone upstairs to throw on some makeup and check e-mail. Oh, there had been that weird e-mail I deleted without reading.

The subject line was "One Dead Turkey"— I thought it was another ad for Viagra. So I had been upstairs for about 20 minutes. Had I locked the door? What difference did that make, since I needed a new lock? Duh.

Dolores looked grim.

"Wanda, we're going to be murdered at the table. I can tell. I have a feeling."

I started to remind her that everybody I had invited was respectable and a known quantity, despite varying degrees of eccentricity, and that it was more likely that a guest would keel over from my cooking, but she cut me off.

"Nobody sends notes like that unless they are a wacko. Somebody is plotting to knock us off one by one."

"Dolores, that's ridiculous," I said, reaching for a glass and the martini pitcher.

"Excuse me?" she shot back. "I am not ending up a statistic in a broken-down little cottage stuck between two freeways."

"Thanks."

"You know what I mean. This place *is* a little isolated." Then she brightened the way she does when she has a brilliant idea of scamming somebody into hiring me. "What if this property is worth something? What if somebody wants to scare you into selling?"

"I'd sell in a minute if somebody made a serious offer," I sighed.

"Okay"— she ran a hand through her magenta spikes,

which messed up the effect, but made her seem more human —"we have to outsmart the murderer."

"What murderer?" I squawked. "There's been no murder. Unless you count the turkey."

"That was just the first step," she said darkly. "We're next."

We sat in silence for a moment, chewing on ice cubes.

"Okay, this is what we are going to do," Dolores finally said in her take-charge agent voice. "We have to knock off the suspects."

I gasped.

"Since we don't know which one of them left the turkey," she continued, "we have to incapacitate all of them, and then beat a confession out of the guilty party."

Dolores was sounding like a really bad television script. There is a reason why *Law and Order* wins Emmies, and it is because the writers never come up with stuff like that.

"Whoa," I said. "I am not bashing anybody over the head."

"Who said bash? We're going to drug them."

"With what?" Somehow I had quickly fallen into her demented train of thought, a Pavlovian response that happens to anybody who has ever had an agent on whom one's income depends.

She rummaged in her large purple tote bag. "I must have something." Eventually, all she could come up with were two vials of eye drops, some stale-dated nasal spray, an empty bottle of Prozac, an airplane-issue Drambuie, assorted painkillers, a small hot-water bottle, and a suspiciously wrinkled hand-rolled cigarette.

She pulled on her shoes, despite Meow Meow being attached to one of them, and we climbed upstairs to examine my medicine cabinet. I had the usual: decongestants, pain relievers, weird First Nations liniments, and an assortment of herbal relaxants. (I lead a stressful life, between auditions, no auditions, and sexual harassment, to say nothing of bills, bills, bills.)

Dolores's eyes lit up when she saw the three bottles of St. John's Wort. "Perfect! This will knock them out!"

I wasn't sure I wanted to knock anybody out, but by now she had convinced me there was Danger Afoot. She put the bottles in her pocket just as the doorbell rang.

We clumped downstairs and opened the door. Serena stood eye to eye with the turkey, looking at it angrily. "Is this supposed to be funny?"

"What?"

Serena had so many grudges hanging around, despite her generally charming disposition, that I couldn't keep track. Suddenly I remembered an old review that had made an unfortunate reference to her hairdo and turkey feathers.

"This is not funny."

"This has nothing to do with you," I said. "Somebody left this for me."

"Oh," she said, ducking under the turkey and handing

me a bottle of wine. "Sorry." She kissed me on the cheek and held out her arms for Meow Meow, who jumped into a cuddle and licked her face. Darned dog would do anything to make me feel inadequate.

Just as I was about to close the door, Arnie pulled up in his pickup. He stomped through the snow to the door, stared at the turkey, and said, "Very funny." I wracked my brain. What obscure item in our past had the turkey triggered? That he had taken me to a turkey dinner at his parents 20 years ago, which had ended any hint of romance between us? (That can happen when a man's mother pulls him onto her lap and tries to spoon-feed him in the middle of dinner.)

More vehicles pulled up in my tiny lane. This was going to be waaay too stressful if every guest had an issue with the turkey, when in fact it was *my* turkey, *my* threat, *my* issue. I hissed to Dolores, "Do it!"

As I greeted Gil and Nancy, I glanced sideways into the kitchen and saw Dolores breaking open the first bottle of St. John's Wort, pounding the tablets with my rolling pin (used only for decoration until now), then hauling open the oven door and sprinkling the powder into the inside of the turkey. When Michael arrived, she was into the second bottle and onto the yams. Unfortunately, she was hitting a lot more than the pills, and I brilliantly surmised that no pumpkin pie was going to be happening at this dinner. And when Lillian tottered in the door with her walker, followed by Bajan, her chauffeur for the day, Dolores was into the third bottle and the mashed potatoes, her magenta dress now splotted with orange. She even sprinkled some on the salad, bless her. That should fix them, all these demented killers who had come to dinner.

* * *

Two hours later, Dolores and I, who had been careful not to eat more than a spoonful of any dish, stared at each other triumphantly. Arnie was face down in his mashed potatoes. Serena was leaning back in her chair, nose to the ceiling, snoring. (That was very satisfying.) Gil and Nancy were cuddled together, breathing nasally. Michael had slid out of his chair (he had drunk enough wine to pass out on his own) and was under the table, where Meow Meow was chewing on the leather loafers I had bought him as a birthday present five years ago. Bajan was sitting upright in his chair, eyes wide open, breathing deeply in a Zen sort of way. Lillian had also slid onto the floor, taking the turkey carcass and part of the table setting with her.

Dolores gave me the thumbs-up, and I flashed two thumbs back.

"Change of plan. Now we call the police," she said, reaching for the phone. It rang as she put her hand on it, and she recoiled.

I grabbed the phone. "Yes?"

"Enjoying the dead turkey?" said a loud, weird voice

that penetrated all the way to where Dolores was sitting. I looked at Dolores, my eyes wide.

The line clicked off.

"I think we might have jumped to some conclusions," I said weakly, but then Dolores, my kick-ass agent, looked at me, made a funny noise, and fainted. She landed in a magenta heap, her purple pumps blocking the doorway.

I ran to her and tried to revive her, slapping her wrists and all the other stuff I learned playing nurses in movies of the week, while Meow Meow licked her face.

The front door knob rattled. I grabbed the phone and dialled 411. No, rats. Start over. I hung up and dialled 911.

I knew it was too late but screamed anyway, with all the vocal power I could muster after the years of pricey vocal training that had gone to waste in low-budget thrillers. "Help! We're going to be murdered!"

I screamed my address into the phone and screamed some more. I heard footsteps in the hall, knew whoever it was would be coming around the corner, and I kept screaming. It was very therapeutic but not helpful. Everybody at the table was passed out, and Dolores wasn't coming out of her stupid faint anytime soon.

My eyes were glued to the hallway. I grabbed the nearest thing I could find to protect myself — an inadequate statuette for best performance by a vegetable in a national commercial. At least I would go down fighting.

A glimpse of a large boot made me hoist the statuette

like an axe, and then the rest of the body followed. When I saw a bit of blue hair, I knew who it was.

Brad came around the corner, grinning.

"Hey, babe," he said smugly. "And you said I didn't have a sense of humour."

As he looked around the room at the dining table and all the comatose guests, his smile began to fade. His jaw dropped and his eyes turned into big cymbals, but he continued with what must have been a rehearsed speech. "I thought you might get a kick out of a different sort of Christmas turkey."

He was staring so hard at the passed-out mess of dinner guests that he stumbled over Dolores's purple pump. Dolores moaned softly, still out on the floor like a flattened plum.

Meow Meow began to snarl at him, her magenta fangs bared.

"Remember how you said we should quit seeing each other cold *turkey?*" He emphasized the last word as if he were the world's greatest wit. "Well, I thought it would be sort of, like, a funny metaphor ... if ...," he droned on.

Meow Meow emitted a murderous woof and leaped at him. I knew Meow Meow and figured I would have another dead turkey in my possession if I didn't step in. I ran and grabbed at her purple doggie hair, but it was slick with dye and I couldn't get a grip.

The three of us careened around the room, knocking over my best vintage lamp, a wicker plant stand, and (really unfortunate) the bowl of marbles. Meow Meow's teeth were in

Brad's hair. My hands were scrabbling around Meow Meow's neck. We crashed against the window, pulling the drapes down, then, our feet rolling on the marbles, ricocheted back into the martini pitcher, drenching ourselves.

The sirens were wailing when I finally pulled Meow Meow off Brad. He was missing most of his blue highlights, and half of his T-shirt was gone. But the hair would grow back, and the T-shirt was a freebie from a Nickelback concert.

I collapsed back onto the dining table with doggie dearest in my arms. Darned dog kept wriggling and trying to get at Brad while spitting out bits of blue hair like confetti. She bit at my Lillian sweater, which began to unravel big time. Too late for modesty. I wrestled with Meow Meow, knocking wineglasses and vegetables to the floor. We thrashed around, leaving long strands of wool and drool over the dishes.

We rolled over Gil and Nancy. We knocked Arnie's face sideways into his potatoes. As we careened past Bajan, he made an "Om" sort of noise. From the floor, Dolores mumbled something that sounded suspiciously like "Oh, Dez, do that again," which made me want to throw up, but I was otherwise engaged.

Brad was now on the floor, whimpering, cursing, and choking on Pekinese hair. His eyes were fixed on Meow Meow, still writhing in my arms. He hauled himself to his feet and lunged toward us, except his first frenetic step landed on about 25 marbles. He went up in the air like Elvis Stojko and landed on the table full speed, sliding to the end, knocking himself out cold on the huge bowl of yams. Bits of dressing flew up into the air and landed on the table like little brown hailstones.

Meow Meow and I were still locked in a death grip usually known only to professional wrestlers. Getting her little fangs into one of the few remaining loose pieces of yarn hanging from my tattered sweater, she pulled. I fought back, but that only made it worse.

The sirens howled to a stop in front of my house.

The magenta monster gave a nasty little woof of triumph, grabbed the last piece of yarn in her fangs, and whizzed over to nestle in the crook of Dolores's arm. I watched the yarn whipping across the room, over the Last Christmas Supper tableau of passed-out guests, suddenly aware of the breeze from the doorway. I looked down at myself in horror.

I guess I must have taken a few moments to absorb my state of undress, for when I looked up, 10 cops in SWAT gear, 3 paramedics with medical cases, and 2 guys with TV cameras were in my doorway, staring at the room.

And at me.

I swear I heard Meow Meow purr.

About the Author:

Linda Kupecek is the author of *Rebel Women: Achievements Beyond the Ordinary,* and *The Rebel Cook: Entertaining Advice for the Clueless,* both from Altitude Publishing. The holiday stories in *Fiction and Folly for the Festive Season* are loosely based on hearsay, news reports, unsubstantiated gossip and family history, and are embellished with much of her imagination. All she can confirm is that sometime in Alberta over the past seventy years, a party nearly split a house in two; an elderly man played a harmonica in a homeless shelter; a group of people passed out at Christmas dinner; and the Salvation Army helped a family in need.

Author's Acknowledgments:

Many thanks to Diana Schwenk of the Mustard Seed Street Ministry in Calgary for her generous assistance with background information and in answering my many questions. If, after reading "Harmonica for the Homeless," you are moved to make a donation to this fine organization, the address is: The Mustard Seed Street Ministry, 102 11 Avenue SE, Calgary, Alberta, T2G 0X5. There are homeless shelters (which also accept donations) in most cities. If, after reading "Angels in the Valley," you are inspired to donate to the Salvation Army, another noble organization, you can find the contacts in the telephone directory in your city or town. If, after reading the